SPELLSTOPPERS

CAT GRAY

USBORNE

1

Max had a problem. A big problem – the sort that ruins your life. Over time, Max had learned to expect the worst, because in his experience, the worst nearly always happened. But it was hard to feel like that today. The summer holidays had just begun, the sun was shining, and Max rushed downstairs, two at a time.

He went through his usual routine to make breakfast. He got his wooden spoon, and used it to turn the kettle on. Then he dropped two slices of bread into the toaster, using the edge of the spoon to press down the lever. The fridge was harder to manage without touching it, but Max had got pretty good with the wooden spoon. He'd had years of practice. Avoiding anything that used electricity was almost second nature to him, but he always needed to be on his guard. If he ever relaxed, disaster inevitably followed.

Max took out the milk and butter, careful not to let his hand brush against the inside of the fridge. It had only been six months since he had broken the last one. He could feel his mother's eyes on him as he prodded the door closed. She was always watching him, as if she was waiting for him to break something else.

Today, she seemed even more anxious than usual. She kept glancing out of the window, into the street, and was twisting a set of keys round and round her finger.

"I've got something to tell you," she said, as she watched Max butter his toast, then smother it in peanut butter. "You might not like it."

Max was immediately suspicious.

"We're not going on holiday again, are we?"

"No! Not after the last one."

She was referring to the time she had tried to take Max on an aeroplane, before either of them realized how bad his problem was. After he had broken three ticket scanners in a row, the security guards had refused to let Max go any further. Max suspected that was actually a good thing. It had been painful enough getting shocked by the ticket scanners. He'd have probably died if he'd touched something as big as an aeroplane.

"What is it, then?" he asked, through a mouthful of toast.

"Remember that competition I entered? The one where you had to come up with a slogan for that energy company?"

Max nodded. His mother had spent days trying to think of a catchy one-liner. She had literally come up with hundreds of ideas. He couldn't blame her – the first prize had been forty thousand pounds.

"Well, I won," she said.

"That's brilliant!" cried Max, leaping to his feet. "We're rich!"

But his mother was shaking her head.

"I won second prize. A new car. It arrived this morning."

"What's wrong with that?" asked Max. "We've never been able to afford a car before!"

"It's electric," she said. "An electric car. I'm so sorry, Max."

Max felt the excitement that had bubbled up inside him fade away, and a feeling of despair crept into its place. He rarely travelled in cars of any sort, but a brand-new electric car sounded particularly dangerous.

"But if I touch anything electric, it breaks."

"It'll be okay," said his mother, reaching forwards and taking his hand. "I've worked out a way around it.

You just need to put on your wellies and your special gloves."

"But it's boiling!"

"Please, Max. Just give it a try. We could go off on a trip somewhere – wouldn't that be fun?"

Max sighed, then went over to the coat rack in the hall. He shoved his bare feet into his black rubber boots, which already felt hot and sticky. Then he picked up his "special gloves" and felt even worse. They weren't special at all. They were just ordinary rubber washing-up gloves. He hated them more than anything, but he often had to wear them in public, especially if they went on a train or a bus. That was dreadful. No one wore wellington boots in London, especially when it wasn't even raining, and rubber gloves just made you look strange. It might have been bearable if they had been black, like his boots, but the only ones in the supermarket that were small enough for Max were bright yellow, just to make it extra-obvious that he was wearing washing-up gloves. He hated the powdery feel of them and their horrible, sweet smell. They reminded him of how weird he was.

It hadn't always been like this. Up until Max was eight, he had been completely ordinary. He could change the channels of the television without breaking it and he

8

was able to touch household appliances without using a wooden spoon. Then, soon after his eighth birthday, he had been at his friend Sami's house playing a video game, when suddenly he felt a sharp stab of pain in his fingers and the games console had died. No one could revive it. Sami's father had suggested that they use his old one instead, but as soon as it was Max's turn, the same thing happened. Both Sami and his parents had gone a bit silent after that, and the next day in class Sami ignored him completely.

Similar things started happening at school too – there was an incident with the lights at the Christmas concert, a full-on disaster in the computer room, and within six months Max had gone from having lots of friends to having no one at all. Now people seemed to sense that there was something wrong with Max just by looking at him. Although it had only been four years since his problem started, it felt like an eternity. He had never heard of anybody else reacting to electricity in the same way. Even the doctor couldn't explain it. It was as if he was cursed.

"Come on!" cried his mother, hurrying past him, carrying a large, bulging plastic bag.

Max followed her down the front steps and out onto

the street. The new car was parked right in front of their house. It was black and shiny, and his mother stroked it gently, as if it was a horse or a cat.

"Don't look so worried," she said. "You've been in cars before and it's been fine."

"Yes, but there wasn't a giant battery sitting underneath those cars, was there?"

"I've thought it all through," said his mother, firmly. She opened the door on the passenger side, then pulled a large rubbery sheet out of the plastic bag. "I'll just spread this over the seat and then you'll be completely safe."

Max stared at the sheet in horror. It was the kind of thing that you put on beds to stop people weeing on them.

"I can't sit on that," he croaked. "People will think I wet myself."

"Don't be silly," she said. "It's the most practical solution."

She went around the car and got into the driver's seat.

"Get in!" she called, leaning over towards him with an encouraging smile.

Max climbed into the car. He sank down into the rubber-covered seat, which made a gentle farting noise as he lowered himself into it. The sheet smelled just like the washing-up gloves and it stuck to the bare skin of his arms, below the short sleeves of his T-shirt.

"See?" said his mother, beaming at him. "It's all fine. So, where do you want to go? You choose."

"The beach," said Max, at once. He loved the sea, but as they lived in London, he hardly ever got a chance to see it.

"It's a bit far," said his mother, looking doubtful, but then she caught sight of Max's eager face.

"All right," she said. "Let's do it."

Max felt his spirits soar. The new car was actually quite nice. Everything looked expensive and shiny, and there were lots of screens everywhere, which lit up as soon as the motor was switched on.

Max settled back into his rubbery cocoon, wishing that it wasn't so hot. He was sweating already and it was only nine o'clock in the morning.

"Can we turn the air conditioning on?" he asked. His mother frowned at the dashboard, looking confused.

"I don't know how," she said. "Why don't you have a look at the instruction manual? It's in the glove compartment, just in front of you."

Max reached forwards to open it. He was wearing his rubber gloves so he knew he'd be okay. But he wasn't quite careful enough. His elbow grazed the side of the door and brushed against the controls for opening and shutting the window. The moment his bare skin touched the control panel there was a loud bang. Pain seared through Max's body, shooting up his arm and into his chest. He had just enough time to register what had happened before he blacked out.

2

"Max?" He heard his mother's voice, close to his ear. She sounded scared. "Max?"

He wasn't sure exactly how long he'd been unconscious. It might have only been a couple of seconds, or it could have been a few minutes. He opened his eyes and saw he was still in the car, with his mother leaning over him. She let out a sigh of relief when she saw he was awake.

"Are you okay?" she asked.

Max nodded.

"Thank heavens for that."

She slumped back against her seat and started crying.

Max watched her, and felt a lump rise in his own throat.

"Is the car all right?" he asked, hoping that somehow he hadn't broken it.

His mother tried to start it up. Nothing happened. She tried again and again, but the car was completely dead. Max was expecting her to be angry, but she just looked upset and frightened, and that was even worse. Her whole body seemed to sag with unhappiness, as if the situation had crumpled her up. Max had never seen his mother look so defeated. He didn't know what to say to comfort her, so they both sat there in an awkward, uncomfortable silence that seemed to grow bigger the longer it lasted.

"Let's go back inside," she said, eventually. "Will you be able to walk? Are you sure you're not hurt?"

"I'm fine," he insisted, even though he still felt sick from the electric shock. "Honestly."

Max trudged back into the house, and tore off his boots and gloves, resisting his mother's attempts to help him. His arms and legs felt prickly and weak, and he was so dizzy that the hallway seemed to rock gently, as if he was on a boat. But that was nothing compared to the fact that he'd destroyed his mother's brand-new car. She was calling the garage now, but still watching him anxiously, as if she was afraid he'd faint again.

As Max suspected, the people from the garage were not able to fix the car. They had never seen anything like it, apparently. They kept questioning Max's mother, and although she was careful not to mention anything about Max, he could tell that they were suspicious.

"You must have done something," they kept saying. "Everything's short-circuited, and the battery looks like it's melted. It's impossible."

When they finally left, Max looked at his mother, who seemed even more defeated than she had done before.

"I'm really sorry about the car."

"It doesn't matter," she said heavily. "As long as you're all right."

"I told you – I'm fine," he said, trying to sound like he meant it.

"We can't go on like this though, Max. At some point, you're going to get seriously hurt."

"I know!" cried Max, frustration welling up inside him. "But it keeps happening – I can't stop it!"

"And it's getting worse," said his mother. Her voice cracked like she was about to burst into tears again. She closed her eyes for a minute, as if she was trying hard to pull herself back together.

"Could you go upstairs to your room for a bit?" she said, at last. "I need to think about what we can do to fix this problem. Something we haven't tried…"

"I'll be more careful…" he began, but she cut him off, her voice still wobbly and upset.

"Please, Max."

He went up to his room, still feeling awful. It seemed impossible that just two hours ago they had been planning to go to the beach. Everything felt wrong and horrible. He could hear his mother pacing up and down the sitting room, directly below him, for what seemed like hours, and he was sure he heard her weeping again. Then he heard her speaking to somebody on the phone. He pressed his ear to the floorboards, and although he couldn't make out what she was saying, he could tell from her tone of voice that it didn't bode well.

Much later, she came upstairs and knocked on his door. She wasn't crying any more, which was good, but her face was still blotchy and she looked exhausted.

"Your grandfather's coming over soon," she said. "He's driving up from Yowling."

"Why?" asked Max. He knew practically nothing about his grandfather beyond the fact that he existed and lived somewhere in the countryside. He'd never even met him. Max had always wanted to be part of a bigger family, but it had only ever really been him and his mother.

"Because..." His mother stopped and took a deep breath. "Because I've been speaking to him and we both agreed it would be a good idea if you went and stayed with him for a while."

"What?" Max leaped up from his bed in horror. "You're getting rid of me?"

"Of course not! It's just for the summer holidays. But you've got to learn how to control this problem you have with electricity – you can't go on like this. And your grandfather is the only person who'll be able to help."

At that moment, the doorbell buzzed.

"That'll be him now," she said, and went to answer it.

"I don't get it," said Max, as he followed her down the stairs. "He doesn't even know me – how's he going to be able to help?"

But his mother had already tugged open the front door and Max saw his grandfather standing on the doorstep.

You could tell just by looking at him that he didn't belong in London – he was too wild and messy. He was tall with wispy grey hair, thick grey eyebrows and an unruly grey beard. His clothes were particularly odd –

17

his shirt was singed and torn badly at the cuffs, his trousers were patched at the knees, while his brown leather boots were blackened with scorch marks. It looked as if he'd been caught up in some sort of explosion, or fight, or possibly both. He grinned when he saw Max peering nervously at him from the hall.

"Another chip off the old block," he said, striding inside and clapping Max so hard on the back that he almost fell over.

"Max, this is your grandad," announced his mother.

"Hello," said Max, not sure what to make of him.

"First off, you're not calling me Grandad," said his grandfather. "My name's Bram."

"Okay," said Max uncertainly.

His mother sighed, but Bram didn't seem to notice. He carried on talking to Max as if Max knew exactly what was going on.

"You packed yet? We need to get back. Got a long drive ahead."

"No," said Max, and he turned to his mother.

"Do I have to go?" he pleaded desperately. He wasn't at all sure about going off with someone he didn't know, even if it was his grandfather.

"Yes," said his mother, more firmly now. "You get

your things together, and Bram and I will have a little chat."

Max did as she said. He didn't feel at all happy about the situation, but there didn't seem to be any alternative. If Bram really could help him, it was worth a shot.

He trudged upstairs and stood in the middle of his bedroom, wondering what he should take. His tiny room was crammed with books – mainly thick, dull volumes about history and science and geography. There was even a set of fat encyclopaedias, with muddy brown covers. It wasn't that Max liked reading these sorts of books, it was because he couldn't just look things up on the internet, which often made homework difficult.

A half-made model of a ship lay on his desk beside his school things, but Max knew that he couldn't fit it inside his rucksack without breaking it. Instead, he just grabbed a random selection of clothes, a pair of pyjamas and his toothbrush, then went downstairs to retrieve his wooden spoon from the kitchen. He'd definitely need that. His grandfather raised his bushy eyebrows when he saw Max shoving a spoon into his rucksack, but he said nothing.

"That reminds me," said his mother, getting to her feet. "Don't forget your special gloves." She picked up the washing-up gloves from where Max had thrown them down earlier and held them out.

"He won't need those," said Bram, glaring at the gloves as if they had offended him. "You can keep them."

"I have to wear them," said Max, gearing himself up to explain. But his grandfather drank the last of his tea and stood up, seizing Max's rucksack and slinging it over his own shoulder.

"Right, we'll be off," he said. "Don't worry, Emily, he'll be fine."

But Max's mother was looking as if she'd had a change of heart. She held Max by the shoulders and looked very intently at her father, as if she was trying to read his mind.

"You have stopped working for the Keeper, haven't you?" she asked. "There's no chance that Max will get mixed up in any of that?"

"Course not," he said. "He'll be as safe as can be."

"Who's the Keeper?" asked Max, looking from Bram to his mother. "And can someone tell me what's happening?"

His mother looked helplessly at Bram.

"You'll have to explain," she said. "I've never told him anything. I don't know how to begin."

"I'll start on the drive down," said Bram. "No point hitting him with it all at once. He won't believe me anyway. Not until he sees it for himself."

Max was more confused than ever. He glanced down at the peculiar scorch marks on Bram's boots then frowned suspiciously up at his grandfather, who grinned back at him, showing a mouthful of crooked brown teeth.

Max was not entirely sure where Yowling was, but it seemed to be a long way away. They had rattled through London in his grandfather's ancient van, which spluttered and wheezed so loudly you had to shout if you wanted to make yourself heard. The only good thing was that it was so low-tech, Max felt like there was less chance that he'd accidentally break it. The van would probably break down all on its own, especially given how fast his grandfather was driving. Now they were on the motorway, they were speeding along so quickly that the landscape was blurring and the engine was emitting a piercing, rusty scream.

"I heard what happened," yelled Bram, above the noise. "With the new car."

"I can't help breaking things!" Max shouted back. "I didn't mean to wreck it."

"I know!" replied Bram. "I'm the same. If I touch anything electric, I frazzle it. Always been like that. That's why Emily rang me. She knew I'd be able to help."

"You have it too?" Max turned to look at him in surprise.

"Yep," said Bram. "Runs in the family."

Max was stunned. "I thought it was just me. Why didn't anyone tell me before?"

"To begin with, your mother was hoping you wouldn't have it," said Bram. "And when it became clear you did, she knew I'd get involved, and she doesn't really approve of me."

"But why doesn't she have it too? If it runs in the family?"

"It often skips a generation," said Bram. "Bit unfortunate, really. My parents didn't have it either, but my grandmother did. Makes it tricky when it comes to handing down the family business."

"What sort of business—" he began, but Bram cut him off.

"Plenty of time to talk about all that later," he said. "First off, let's get back to Yowling. You need to be there to understand."

Bram started to whistle tunelessly, but Max's head

was bursting with about a million questions. Something odd was going on and he wanted to know what it was. He wasn't sure whether he was feeling apprehensive or excited. Either way, he wished that they'd get to Yowling a bit sooner so he could finally find out.

"Nearly there," announced Bram at last, and Max jerked awake.

He'd fallen asleep with his face pressed uncomfortably against the window, and his neck was stiff and sore. The van had slowed now, and was making an exhausted gurgling sound as they trundled along a narrow bumpy road that sloped steeply downwards. Max leaned forwards as he caught a glimpse of the sea, far below him, and realized that they had come as far as the coast. The evening sun made the water shimmer with a warm yellow glow, and cast long strange shadows.

There was a loud cawing cry, and something swooped through the air across the cliffs and glided for a moment beside the car. It was a huge bird, its wings impossibly long, its feathers dark and gleaming.

"Look," called Max, pointing at the shape silhouetted against the sky. "It's an eagle!"

Bram glanced at it, then set his jaw and tightened his grip on the steering wheel.

"That's not an eagle," he said. "That's an owl."

Max watched as it flew off across the waves, towards a large, turreted building that seemed to be sitting in the middle of the bay, completely surrounded by the sea. All the dark pointed towers made it look jagged and sharp against the fat golden clouds.

"What's that?" he said, pointing.

"Yowling Castle," said Bram curtly. "Horrible place. Full of owls – and worse."

"I thought owls lived in woods," said Max, feeling a prickle of unease as he stared at the huge dark castle. "Do they even like the sea?"

"These ones do," said Bram. "We're coming into Yowling now," he added, abruptly changing the subject.

A little village was ranged around the edge of the beach. White-washed buildings huddled into the steep cliffs around a small sandy cove. But before they got any closer, Bram turned the van sharply to the right, chugged up a narrow lane, then pulled into what looked like a very ramshackle farmyard. A couple of chickens squawked in alarm and rushed into the darkness of a nearby barn.

"Here we are," said Bram, as the van screeched to a halt in the middle of the yard. "Home at last."

Although Bram seemed pleased that the long journey was over, Max felt distinctly apprehensive as he looked around at his unfamiliar new surroundings. He was about as far from home as he'd ever been in his life.

3

The first thing that Max noticed as he stepped out of the van was a painted wooden sign on the weathered brick wall.

Harrow and Co.
Spellstopping and Non-Magical Repairs

Harrow was his family's surname, but it was the second part that really interested him. He reread the sign, because it sounded so peculiar, then turned around to ask Bram about it. But his grandfather had vanished.

Max scanned the farmyard, which was surrounded by a set of low stone buildings that all faced each other. Bits of old machinery were piled up haphazardly in the corner next to a barn, and grass grew in the cracks between the worn paving stones. There was a light on in one of the outbuildings, which shone through the dusty, cobwebbed windows. Then Max spotted Bram, who had marched off in the opposite direction and was pulling open the farmhouse door. Three large black dogs spilled out of it, barking loudly.

"Come on!" yelled Bram over the noise.

Max hurried after him into the house, and was immediately swamped by the dogs. They all jumped up at him at once, putting their paws on his chest and trying to lick his face as he struggled his way inside.

"Down!" said Bram, and they reluctantly backed off and sat by Max's feet instead.

"I don't mind," said Max, as he patted each one of them in turn.

"That one's Treacle," said Bram, pointing to a dog who was greying around its muzzle. "She's the mother of the other two. The one whose tongue is always hanging out is called Sardine and the one with a white spot on his back is Banana."

"Banana?"

"I named them after their favourite foods," said Bram, matter-of-factly. "Although I obviously didn't set out to give Treacle any treacle. She discovered that by herself."

He let out a sudden snort of laughter, clearly

remembering some treacle-related incident, but Max was distracted by the kitchen. It wasn't like any other kitchen he'd ever seen. There was no cooker, or kettle, or toaster, just a big cast-iron range that stood in the corner, radiating heat, with a huge basket of logs beside it. An old oak table took up most of the middle of the room, and a wooden dresser was crammed with mismatched plates and mugs. The remaining floor space was mostly given over to dog beds. Max went over to the range and examined it.

"It doesn't use electricity," he said, pleased with his discovery.

"I do my best to avoid it," said Bram. "There's electric light, a washing machine and a telephone, but that's about it. No sense in going mad with electricity if you're a spellstopper. Best to save your energy for more important things."

"What's a spellstopper?" asked Max, intrigued by the unfamiliar word. "And why was it on that sign?"

"I'll tell you about spellstopping once you've unpacked," said Bram, ignoring Max's eager expression. "First off, I need to make dinner."

Bram unhooked a large metal pot, which had been hanging on the wall, and banged it down on the stove.

Then he started hunting about the kitchen. He seized a turnip which was sitting in a fruit bowl on the table, a couple of limp carrots which were lying on the dresser, and a handful of potatoes which had been left in the sink. He dropped all of the vegetables into the pot and poured water on them, then carried on wandering about the kitchen, as if searching for more ingredients.

"What are you making?" asked Max, eyeing the pot with suspicion. His mother normally gave him pasta for dinner, because she knew that he liked it. She was a good cook, and usually went out of her way to make dishes that Max would enjoy. He had a feeling that Bram's approach to mealtimes was somewhat different.

"Stew," replied Bram. "Stick anything into a pot and boil it for long enough and it'll turn into a stew eventually. Aha!"

He snatched a small plastic bag from the windowsill, ripped it open, and tipped some chunks of greenish meat into the bubbling mixture. Max wanted to ask how long the meat had been sitting there, but stayed quiet. He wondered if his mother knew what she'd let him in for.

Suddenly, there was a very loud bang. The windows rattled, and a plate fell off the dresser and smashed on the stone floor. Max jumped, but Bram didn't look surprised. He ambled across the room and bent down to pick up the pieces.

"Sounds like Kit's having a bad time out there," he said, putting the shards of china on the table. "I'll see if I can glue that back together tomorrow."

"Who's Kit?" asked Max, peering out of the window and across the yard. The explosion seemed to have come from the building opposite the house – the one with the light in the window.

"You'll meet her soon enough," said Bram.

Max could see wisps of smoke coming out from underneath the door. Whoever Kit was, Max was not entirely sure if she was still alive.

"I'll go out and see what's happened," he said, keen to know the reason behind the explosion.

"Don't bother," said Bram. "She'll be finished before long – no point in disturbing her. Go upstairs, get settled, unpack your things. That bag of yours is getting in the way."

For a moment, Max considered rushing outside anyway. He wanted to find out what was going on. But he wasn't sure how his grandfather would react. The last thing he wanted was to annoy Bram before he'd even got to know him, especially if he was supposed to stay with him all summer.

With a sigh, he picked up his rucksack and went out of the kitchen into the passage beyond.

"Up the stairs and the second door to the left," Bram yelled after him. "It's the room with the pink wallpaper."

The hallway was very dark, with big wooden beams and a low ceiling. The stairs creaked loudly with each step Max took. Upstairs, he counted the doors in the narrow corridor and pushed open the second one on the left.

His first thought was that the room smelled musty, as if nobody had stayed in it for a very long time. His second impression was that it was extremely pink and tidy – not at all like the rest of the dark, cluttered house. The wallpaper was rose pink, and so were the bed sheets, the curtains, and even the carpet. Posters of pop stars were stuck up on the walls, yellowed with age, and a dressing table with an oval mirror stood next to the window. For a moment, Max frowned at the sea of pink that surrounded him, unable to find a reason for it, then realized, with a sudden shock, that this must have been his mother's old bedroom. It was an odd feeling, coming across a version of her that he had never known about, and Max realized that she had never told him a single thing about her childhood, except for the fact that she was an only child, just like him.

31

Max plonked his bag down and pulled open the wardrobe. There was a glittery pair of shoes in it, but aside from that it was empty. Max couldn't be bothered with coat hangers so he just stuffed all his things onto the shelves instead. The wooden spoon went on his bedside table – he'd need it for the light switch later.

The room was stuffy and hot, so Max opened the small casement window, pushing at the glass until it juddered open with a rusty squeak. He could see over the rooftops of the houses in the nearby village and across the bay, to where the spiky outline of the castle dominated the horizon. The more he stared at it, the stranger it seemed. Wreaths of green mist clouded about the base of its dark stone walls, so the castle looked as if it was hovering above the water. Tiny silhouettes of birds flitted around the turrets in the fading light and Max wondered again if they really could be owls. It was odd, seeing so many of them gathered together in one place.

When he went back downstairs, there was a horrible smell of rotten vegetables wafting through the passageway and the kitchen was enveloped in steam. Bram was stirring the stew and a girl with long auburn hair was sitting at the kitchen table.

"Max, meet Kit," said Bram. "Kit's my assistant.

She can mend pretty much anything."

Max stared at the girl, who stared back at him, looking equally curious. She was about the same age as him, and had a friendly sort of face, which was partly covered in freckles, and partly streaked with soot. She was wearing a pair of even sootier overalls, which looked as if they might have been blue originally. One of the sleeves had a large hole in it.

"Go and sit down," instructed Bram. "Dinner's nearly ready."

Max made his way around the dogs, who were grouped about Bram, staring hopefully up at the stew, and sat down at the table next to Kit.

"What happened out there?" he asked eagerly. "I saw the smoke."

But Kit just looked across at Bram, as if she wasn't sure whether or not to answer.

"You can tell Max!" called Bram, still stirring the pot. "He's going to learn the trade. I reckon he'll make a first-rate spellstopper. You should hear about some of the things he's done – he broke an electric car earlier, just by brushing it with his elbow!"

Bram looked at Max proudly. It was an odd feeling, having someone view his problem as a good thing.

But Kit still seemed reluctant to talk.

"Does it happen to you too?" asked Max, trying again. "The electrical thing?"

"No," said Kit. "Bram's the one who does all the spellstopping. I do the non-magical repairs."

"But surely everything's non-magical?" asked Max, who was beginning to feel that nothing made sense any more. "I don't understand. What's spellstopping? And what's it got to do with me?"

"It's the family business," announced Bram, swelling with pride. "We fix magical items. And if they need repairing in the regular way, we do that too. You can't just go and get something mended at any old place if it's magic, can you?"

Max glanced from Bram to Kit, to see if they were joking. They both looked completely earnest.

"But magic doesn't exist," he said, trying to cling on to some semblance of logic.

"Course it does," said Bram firmly. "It's just that most people don't know about it."

Max was beginning to wonder what on earth was going on. He could see now why his mother had kept him away from his grandfather – he was clearly eccentric, to put it mildly.

"So spellstopping literally means stopping spells?" he asked warily, half-expecting Bram and Kit to laugh at how absurd it sounded. But Bram clapped his hands together and beamed, as if Max had just said something extremely clever.

"Got it in one!" cried Bram. "Almost everything we work with was enchanted originally. But sometimes the magic starts going a bit off-kilter, especially if the object's old. I rebalance the magic, so it goes back to working properly. It's a bit like being a doctor, but for magical items. Sometimes I'll remove the magic entirely if it's too dangerous to fix safely – that's where the word spellstopping comes from. Although, in practice, I don't fully spellstop things very often. Customers wouldn't like it, would they? If you're lucky enough to own something magical, why would you want to destroy it? Most of the time, I just fix stuff, so it works like it was supposed to."

Max had absolutely no idea what his grandfather was on about. Kit was nodding along, as if she agreed with everything Bram was saying, but Max was completely mystified.

"So you're telling me that you can do magic?" he croaked.

"Course not!" replied Bram. "Weren't you listening? I'm a spellstopper – that means I can rebalance or eliminate existing magic. Completely different thing. Rare too – I'm the only one in existence. Until you popped up, that is. Can't tell you how pleased I was when Emily rang me. It was the first time she'd ever told me you'd inherited the gift."

Bram gazed at Max fondly. Kit was also watching him, but more cautiously, as if she wasn't quite sure about him yet. The three dogs were staring at him too, their mouths open, their tongues hanging out, as if Max was the most exciting thing they had ever seen. Max rubbed his eyes with the heels of his hands, half expecting to wake up from a particularly vivid dream. When he opened his eyes again, he found that they were all still looking at him. It was very disconcerting.

"You're going to be a spellstopper, Max," announced Bram triumphantly. "I'm sure of it."

Max tried and failed to reply. He was so baffled that he didn't know what to say. It all sounded so far-fetched and peculiar that he wasn't sure if his grandfather was telling the truth or not. Over on the range, the bubbling pot of stew began to make a loud sizzling noise, and Bram sprang up to rescue it.

"It's fine," he said, giving it a hasty stir. "The black bits add flavour."

He carried the vast pot of stew over to the table, his hands encased in a pair of flowery oven gloves.

"Don't worry," he added kindly, seeing Max's baffled expression. "It's a lot to take in all at once."

"Is that why Mum sent me down here?" asked Max slowly, still trying to make sense of everything. "To become a spellstopper like you?"

"Course not," replied Bram patiently. "To be honest, she wants nothing to do with it. That's why she kept you in the dark about it all. But she's finally realized that you'll have to learn a bit of spellstopping just for your own good. Otherwise you'll keep knocking yourself out every time you go near an electric current. Untrained spellstoppers never last long. There'd come a time when you'd do yourself a real injury. Or you'd get struck by lightning."

Max remembered how his mother would make him stay inside and wear his rubber boots during a thunderstorm.

"That's why we're so rare," continued Bram. "Even before electricity came along, the ones who hadn't learned how to control themselves kept dying out.

Anyway, enough of all that for now. Have some stew."

He pushed the pot towards Max, who was still struggling with the extraordinary things he had just been told. He scooped up a ladleful absent-mindedly. An assortment of soggy vegetables and a few chunks of pale meat splattered onto his plate.

"You got the turnip," said Bram, peering at Max's dish. "Good for you – that's the best bit."

He took the pot and began to help himself to a large quantity of stew.

"Sure I can't tempt you?" he asked, waving the ladle at Kit, but Kit shook her head.

"I'll go home for dinner," she said. "They'll be waiting for me."

"Kit never eats anything I cook," said Bram. "Can't think why."

Max inspected the stew. It looked and smelled like the contents of a compost bin if you poured boiling water over it. He glanced at Kit, who grinned at him.

"Eat up!" cried Bram, picking up his own knife and fork. He speared a steaming potato and took a bite out of it.

Max tried a mouthful of the watery stew and instantly choked. It tasted even worse than it looked. The combination of hard, uncooked potato and slimy, rotten carrot was unbelievably awful. He wanted desperately to spit it out, but couldn't quite face doing so in front of Bram. He caught Kit's eye again and saw that she was trying hard not to laugh.

Luckily for Max, there was a knock at the kitchen door. The dogs sprang up and started barking, and Bram got stiffly to his feet and went to see who it was. Max used the opportunity to spit the stew back onto his plate, then realized that Kit was watching him.

"Don't worry, I won't tell him," she said.

"Thanks," replied Max, in relief. He had been unsure what to make of Kit, but he was beginning to feel that she was the sort of person he'd like to be friends with. Then he caught sight of the peculiar man standing just outside the door, speaking in a low voice to Bram.

He wore a black silk top hat, pulled down low over his brow. A scarf was wound across the lower half of his face, even though it was the end of July. He was clutching a box to his chest, and with a sudden jolt of surprise, Max saw that his hands were completely wrapped up in dust-coloured bandages. Max stood up to get a better look at the stranger. He wasn't wearing any shoes, and his feet, too, were completely encased in old cloth bandages.

"Sounds pretty straightforward," Bram was saying. "Come back for it tomorrow evening – it should be done by then."

The man said something else – Max strained to hear him, but he was speaking in a very faint, hollow voice, barely more than a whisper – then he handed the cardboard box over to Bram and hurried off.

"Who was that?" asked Max.

"A customer," replied Kit. "They're supposed to stick to opening hours, but they're always showing up at odd times."

"But the bandages…"

"You get all sorts bringing stuff to us," said Bram with a shrug. "Best not to ask customers too many questions – they don't like it. You should be more concerned by what's in here."

He shook the cardboard box and to Max's surprise it started rattling violently, as if it contained something alive. Bram beamed at Max and Kit as he plonked the box down in the middle of the table.

"Well, Max, you're in luck," he said. "Instead of telling you what spellstopping is, we're going to show you. Right now."

He rolled up the sleeves of his shirt and rocked

backwards and forwards on his heels, as if getting ready for a fight. Kit frowned at the box, which was still rattling angrily.

"You should move that out of the way," she said, nodding at Max's dinner. "Things might get a bit messy."

4

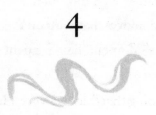

Kit was not exaggerating. Things got very messy, very quickly. Just as Max pushed his plate to one side, he saw that something odd was happening to the cardboard box. A large damp patch appeared in the side of it, and then a jet of steam broke through the soggy cardboard. He peered at it, trying to work out what was going on.

"Stand back!" yelled Bram, and Max flattened himself against the wall, nearly tripping over one of the dog beds.

A round metal object, about the size of a football, exploded out of the box and spun its way across the table, sending plates flying. For a moment, Max froze, thinking that it was a bomb of some sort, but then he saw that it had a black metal handle and a plume of scalding hot steam was coming out of a fat curved spout.

"Is that a *kettle*?" asked Max, staring at it in disbelief. It was the heavy, old-fashioned kind, with no plug or cable, the sort of thing you might find in a junk shop. Max glanced from Bram to Kit, wondering if they found the sight as strange as he did. They were both looking at the kettle with interest, but very little emotion, a bit like how a doctor might examine a patient. Neither of them seemed at all surprised by what was happening.

"How's it doing that?" asked Max. He moved towards it, fascinated, and instantly the kettle gave a loud, shrill shriek and spun away from him.

"I'll get it," said Kit. She sprang forwards and grabbed at the kettle, but it shot violently into the air then crashed down, straight into the pot of stew. Bits of meat and vegetables splattered out in all directions. Bram, who was standing closest to the table, got the worst of it, but Kit and Max also got hit with a sizable portion of tepid stew. It was too much for the three dogs, who began jumping up at them, trying to lick it off.

"EEEEEE!" screamed the kettle, whirling around, spewing steam everywhere.

"Ouch!" cried Max, as a blast of steam went right through his jumper and scalded his arm. He crouched down on the ground, out of the way, and was immediately swamped by the dogs. Sardine seized the opportunity to remove a chunk of meat from Max's hair, while

Treacle and Banana licked his face enthusiastically. Kit looked as if she was about to hurl herself at the kettle again.

"Just leave it be," announced Bram, stepping back from the table. "It'll calm down in a few minutes. In answer to your question, Max, it's doing that because it's enchanted. Not only that, but it's fizzing with unstable magic. And we're going to fix it. Its owner doesn't want us to remove all of the magic – we just need to rebalance it, so it works the way it's meant to."

As he spoke, the kettle's spinning slowed and it finally came to rest on the table, its spout still steaming. Bram edged forwards and seized it by the handle. At once, the kettle started struggling again, but Bram held on to it firmly.

"Look," said Kit, nudging Max. "He's doing it now."

They both watched as Bram clasped the kettle with both hands, an expression of concentration on his face. The jet of steam began to fade, but then Bram suddenly choked and doubled over, coughing violently.

"Are you okay?" asked Max in alarm.

"Fine," spluttered Bram. "Bit of carrot went down the wrong way."

He broke off suddenly as the kettle shrieked and

44

whirled back into life again, twisting out of his hands and flying into the air.

"EEEEEEE!" it screeched, spinning madly as it headed straight for the window.

Bram lunged forwards, still coughing, and tried to grab it, but it was too late. The kettle smashed right through the kitchen window and shot off into the yard.

"Blast," swore Bram, in between coughs.

Max and Kit raced outside, pursued by the dogs.

"It can't have gone far," said Kit, looking around. "It has to be here somewhere."

The two of them hunted all over the yard. Max went inside the gloomy barn, but all he found were bales of musty straw piled up to the wooden rafters, a rusty old trailer, and a couple of sleeping chickens. There was a row of stables, their half doors left open, and Max peered over each one in turn, but saw nothing except a lone mouse scuttling across the cobbled floor. It looked so ordinary and unmagical that doubts began to creep into Max's mind. Could Bram and Kit have really meant what they said about spellstopping? How on earth could it be true? Everyone knew that magic wasn't real. He remembered the kettle, whirling about in mid-air by itself, and frowned.

Max emerged from the stables just in time to see Kit disappear inside the workshop, which was still emitting faint wisps of smoke from the earlier explosion. He hurried after her at once, keen to find out what was in there.

The workshop was extremely untidy and smelled strongly of gunpowder. Perhaps it was the result of the recent accident, but there were bits of furniture and tools lying everywhere. There were pots of polish, dozens of chisels and hammers and metal files, scattered nails and knives and boxes, some of them strewn across the floor, others piled up on the long wooden workbench that ran along the length of the room. On the other side, there was a mass of what looked to Max like junk – old armchairs with their insides coming out, chipped pots, broken toys and a stuffed weasel, mounted on a stand. The weasel caught Max's eye and seemed to smirk at him. Max looked away quickly.

"Can you see the kettle?" asked Kit, who was lifting up dust sheets and peering behind furniture. "It might have hidden itself away in here – I left all the windows open after what happened earlier."

"What did happen earlier?"

Kit pointed at a toy cannon that was sitting on the workbench. It was about twenty centimetres long and looked exactly like a real cannon, but in miniature. Curls of smoke were billowing out of its mouth and drifting through the open window.

"That happened," she said. "I thought Bram had already fixed it, so I decided to polish it up. But as soon as I touched it, it exploded."

"I still don't really get any of this," confessed Max, peering at the cannon. It seemed to be humming slightly, as if it was emitting an electrical charge. He knew instinctively that he didn't want to touch it. "About the spellstopping, I mean."

"Well, you've seen the kettle," said Kit. "Originally it might have been enchanted to do something good, like boil water by itself, or pour out an endless supply of coffee, but the thing about magic is that it isn't stable. It doesn't just stay exactly the same for ever. It's a bit like a car – you have to get it serviced if you want it to carry on running properly."

Max flinched at the comparison. Cars were the last thing he needed to be reminded about.

"Over time, the magic can build up and go bad, so the enchanted object starts acting in a different way from how it was supposed to – that's when people bring whatever it is to Bram."

Max still wasn't convinced.

"If there really are all sorts of magical objects lying around the place, why haven't I heard of them before?"

"Because they're not just lying about," said Kit impatiently. "They're really unusual and valuable, and hardly any of them are owned by regular humans anyway. Of course you wouldn't have come across any."

"Regular humans?" asked Max. "Who else would own these things then?" He gave a short laugh at the sheer ridiculousness of it all, but Kit just shrugged.

"People from the magical community, mostly. Like the people who live in Yowling."

They were interrupted by Bram bursting through the door, accompanied by the three dogs.

"Any luck?" he asked, sounding out of breath.

Max and Kit shook their heads.

"I've checked the vegetable patch and all around the yard. No sign of it. Must have gone further afield."

Bram looked troubled. He kept running his hands absent-mindedly though his grey hair, which was now sticking out madly in all directions.

"What'll the customer say?" he groaned. "You can't replace something like that – it's priceless. My business will be ruined once the word gets round."

"We'll find it," promised Kit, then broke off as the toy cannon began to make a low rumbling noise.

"It's going to blast off again," she said, backing away from the bench. "Can you fix it? Before it goes off?"

Bram sighed and placed his hand on the cannon's metal barrel. For a moment it glowed red and a wisp of smoke curled out of its mouth. Then the smoke faded, the colour returned to normal and Bram took away his hand.

"There," he said, and gave the cannon a gentle shove, so that it rolled towards Kit on its little iron wheels.

Max prodded it gingerly, curious to know what Bram had done.

"So, you've rebalanced the magic?" he asked, picking it up so he could examine it more closely. "Is it back to being a normal toy?"

"Not exactly," said Bram. "Careful…"

But it was too late. Max had pressed a tiny lever at the base of the cannon and with an unexpectedly loud bang, a tiny metal cannonball shot from the cannon's mouth and sped across the workshop with the speed of a bullet, narrowly missing Bram's ear before embedding itself in the wooden door with a loud, splintering thud.

"Seems to be working well enough now," observed Bram calmly, as Max hastily put down the cannon and backed away from it. "That's what it should have done all along."

He looked at Max.

"You'll have to start learning this soon. We need all the help we can get."

"I can start now," said Max eagerly. A whole world of possibilities seemed to have opened up in front of him. After all those years he had spent struggling with electricity, it appeared that there might actually be a good side to what he had only ever thought of as a curse. Up to this point, the prospect of simply using a phone had seemed like an impossible dream. Now Bram was suggesting that he was capable of much, much more. He looked around the workshop, at all the things that were humming with magic, unable to contain the excitement that was bubbling up inside him.

"Too late tonight," said Bram, and ushered them both out of the workshop, much to Max's intense disappointment. "Kit, you need to go home. Do you want a lift?"

"I've got my bike," said Kit, nodding towards the red mountain bike that was propped up against the stone wall. "I'll see if I can spot the kettle on my way back. See you tomorrow."

Kit turned on the bike lights, which made the twilight suddenly seem a lot darker. She gave Max and Bram a cheerful wave then pedalled off down the winding road.

Max's head was still spinning with everything that had happened. He hurried after Bram, who was heading back towards the house, the dogs milling around him. Max had forgotten his earlier doubts and his homesickness – he was too preoccupied with all the things he had just seen, and the wonderful impossibility of it all.

"Bram?" he asked, and his grandfather paused, his hand on the door handle.

"Yep?"

"Did you really mean it – that I could be a spellstopper too?"

Max held his breath as he waited for his grandfather to answer. He still couldn't quite believe that he might have the power to actually influence magic. It sounded too strange and wonderful to be true.

"Course I did," said Bram, and grinned broadly at him. "Just you wait and see."

5

Breakfast the next day was almost as bad as dinner. Max came downstairs, having woken very early. He had been too excited to sleep much, and when he did, his dreams were filled with shrieking kettles, exploding toys and shadowy birds that swooped through a sky as dark as ink. Bram was already in the kitchen, stirring something on the stove. He was using the same large metal pot that he'd used for the stew. The only difference was that this time it was full of something grey and slimy.

"Porridge!" announced Bram, splodging a massive amount of it into a bowl and plonking it onto the table. The porridge was so thick that Max's spoon stuck upright in it. He tried eating a mouthful but it was too gluey, so he put the bowl on the floor while Bram's back was turned, hoping that one of the dogs would eat it for him. They didn't. Treacle ambled over, gave the porridge a sniff, and then walked away without touching it. Sardine and Banana wouldn't even look at it, but just sat in their beds, staring at him reproachfully. Max gave up and put the bowl back on the table before Bram noticed.

Bram was still standing by the stove, his own bowl in his hand, happily eating the claggy porridge, when Kit stuck her head round the door. The dogs immediately leaped up and rushed towards her, their tails wagging madly.

"You've been busy," she said, nodding at the window, and Max realized that the broken pane of glass had already been replaced, as if nothing had ever happened. Bram must have fixed it before Max had come down.

"Has the kettle turned up yet?" she asked.

"Nope," said Bram, between mouthfuls. "Not so much as a whistle."

"How about I take Max into Yowling? Someone might have seen it."

Bram didn't reply. Instead, he frowned at Max as if he was worried about him. Max recognized that look. His mother wore it all the time.

"Please!" he begged. The fact that Bram seemed hesitant made Max want to explore the village more than anything else.

"It's tricky…" mused Bram. He turned to Kit. "What if you run into her? She's been getting worse lately and we don't want her working out who Max is."

"Who?" asked Max, curious.

"The Keeper of Yowling Castle," said Kit. "The current one's called Leandra and everyone in the village is terrified of her. Even my dad gets scared if he catches sight of her. We all just try to keep out of her way."

"What does she do?"

"Sets fire to things, mostly," said Kit. "She can shoot flames from her fingers – it's horrible. She can turn into an owl, too, so you never know when she's going to appear."

"Really?" asked Max, his voice laced with disbelief.

He half-expected Kit to burst out laughing and tell him that it was all a joke. But she and Bram looked completely serious.

"She's part of the castle," said Bram. "Its magic rubbed off on her – gave her powers no person would normally have."

"She's awful," said Kit. "But we should be fine at this time of day. They'll all be back at the castle."

"There's more of them?" asked Max, appalled. "More Keepers like Leandra?"

"Not exactly," said Bram. "There's only ever one Keeper at a time. But when they die, they transform permanently into an owl. All the Keepers, past and present, are bound to the castle – none of them are able to go more than a kilometre or two away from it."

"So the owl I saw yesterday – was that one of them?"

"You saw an owl?" interrupted Kit, looking interested. "Was it Leandra or one of the others?"

"Leandra," said Bram curtly, frowning now. "I'd recognize her anywhere."

"She's after Bram," said Kit helpfully. "She's been trying to get him to spellstop the castle for her, but he won't."

"Of course I'm not going to help her again!" bellowed Bram, and he slammed his hand down on the table with such force that his bowl of porridge shuddered.

Max looked at his grandfather in alarm. It was the first time he'd seen him lose his composure. Bram caught his eye, and seemed to pull himself together. When he next spoke, it was in a deliberately cheerful voice.

"There's no need for you to go into Yowling, Max. There's plenty for you to do here."

"But I'd like to!" exclaimed Max. However dangerous the village might be, the idea of missing out on an adventure was too much for him to bear, especially if magic might be involved. And, although he'd never say it out loud to Bram, he really wanted to get a better look at the castle. He gazed desperately at Bram, willing him to let him go.

"Max has to see Yowling!" cried Kit. "If Max is going to learn spellstopping, he's got to see more of the magical world. Otherwise how will he understand?"

"All right," said Bram, relenting. "Just keep your wits about you and listen to Kit. Her family's lived in Yowling for years without coming to any harm."

Max scrambled up from the table before Bram had time to change his mind.

"You've picked an interesting time to visit," said Kit, as they left the farmyard through the old stone gateposts and went down the steeply sloping lane. "Leandra, the Keeper, is determined to make Bram fix the castle and Bram swears he won't help her. Meanwhile the castle's falling apart – it's all anyone in the village can talk about."

"How could Bram work on something as big as a castle?" asked Max. "It's huge, isn't it?"

"He's done it before, I think," said Kit. "Apparently the Keepers have always relied on spellstoppers to help them keep the castle going. It's enchanted – that's why there's all that green mist around it."

"Have you ever been inside?"

"No! Nobody has for years and years except the Keepers. And Bram, I suppose, but he won't talk about it."

Kit kicked at a loose stone, which rolled down the steep bumpy lane. White clouds of cow parsley lined the grassy verges, and the hedgerows were so green and leafy that Max couldn't see through them.

"Have you always lived in Yowling?" asked Max, curious to know more about Kit.

"For as long as I can remember," said Kit. "There's not that many magical communities around, and we need to be beside the sea because of my dad and my sister."

"Why?"

"Because they're selkies."

"Selkies?" Max was mystified.

"They can turn into seals," she elaborated. "Whenever they go into water."

"What?" Max stopped dead and stared at her. "You're kidding."

"No, I'm not," said Kit irritably. "And before you ask, no, I can't do it too. I don't know why, so don't go on about it."

She sped up, striding along so Max had to hurry after her. He fell into step beside her, and tried to catch her eye, but she ignored him, and so they both marched along in silence. He suddenly caught a familiar smell. It was the sea – he'd know that salty seaweedy tang anywhere.

As they came to the end of the lane and out onto a road, he saw the first glimmer of it. The sun was bouncing off the water, and he heard the squawk of seagulls and the murmur of waves lapping the shore. It was already getting hot, and the sea looked cool and inviting.

"Let's go swimming later," he said to Kit, but she shook her head.

"You really don't want to do that," she said. "All sorts of dangerous creatures live in there. Dad told me. You can't just go splashing around."

Max fell silent, feeling annoyed. What was the point of living next to the sea if you couldn't even paddle?

"Anyway, look – there's the castle," she said, as the cove curved round and the castle suddenly came into view. It was impossible to miss. Although it was set almost a kilometre from the shore, it loomed over the bay. Despite the bright morning sun, it seemed to be in shadow, made even more sinister by the clouds of mist that swirled about it. Behind the castle stood a long line of jagged rocks, which cut the cove off from the sea beyond and gave the whole place a closed-in feeling.

"So the castle is absolutely brimming with magic," continued Kit, warming to the subject. "It's been around for hundreds of years and the village grew up in its shadow. What with the cliffs and the woods and those rocks across the mouth of the cove, Yowling's completely protected from the outside world – it's why so many magical beings live here."

"Can we meet some?" cut in Max. Kit kept saying how magical the village was, but he wanted to see it for himself.

"Of course," said Kit. "We're nearly there."

They were coming up to Yowling now. It had an oddly hushed atmosphere, which reminded Max of the feeling you get very early on a Sunday morning when the whole world seems to be asleep.

As the village was nestled into the side of a cliff, all the houses were at different levels, linked by flights of stone steps. There was a narrow dusty road that ran along the seafront and a small pier that jutted out into the water.

A big pile of lobster pots was stacked up next to the pier, along with an upside-down rowing boat with a nasty splintered chunk taken out of its bottom. Apart from that, the seafront was completely empty.

Max peered at the houses curiously. No two of them were exactly the same. Some were crooked and half-timbered, with odd little windows and high brick chimneys. Others looked like a confused jumble, as if someone had kept adding extra bits onto them as an afterthought. And the very oldest ones were made from pale salt-bleached wood and looked rickety and exhausted, as if they were about to fall down the hill and into the sea.

"This is the main street," said Kit, as they climbed up a steep little street dotted with old shopfronts.

Every single one looked closed, and curtains were drawn across most of the curved bay windows. Max read the faded shop signs – a fishmonger, an apothecary and a sweet shop. He paused to look into the sweet shop, but before he could see inside, an unseen hand quickly pulled the curtain across the window.

"Why isn't anything open?" he asked.

"Everyone's too scared of the Keeper," said Kit. "There's only one shop that's still open in Yowling. That one, over there."

Max looked across the street and saw a bow-fronted

shop with an assortment of buckets and spades, fishing tackle and pet food piled up in the window. Kit went and pressed a little brass doorbell and a few seconds later, there was a buzzing sound as the door unlocked. Max followed Kit inside.

He could see at once that it was an excellent shop. Polished wooden shelves ran around every wall, reaching from floor to ceiling, and stacked with everything you could possibly want. There were bags of flour, pots of jam, packets of nuts, dried fruit and chocolate biscuits. Big glass jars filled with sweets sat next to piles of notebooks and balls of string. However, the more Max looked, the more peculiar things he saw. A jar of dried beetles was placed right next to the sweets. A stack of black candles was arranged upon a shelf. And a cage of live mice sat on the sandy floor next to the shiny mahogany counter. Max had just kneeled down to get a better look at the mice, when he heard a voice speak just above him.

"Some of my customers have unusual tastes," it said.

Max jumped to his feet at once.

A woman was standing behind the counter. Her skin and hair were exactly the same colour as the sandy beach, and her eyes were the soft grey of pebbles. She was wearing a long dress that was a bit like a sack and was the same shade as the rest of her.

"I'm Pearl," she said, and held her hand out to Max. "You must be Bram's grandson."

"How did you know?" asked Max in surprise.

"Yowling is a small place," she said. "And you look like him."

"No I don't," said Max, indignantly, thinking of his grandfather's bushy eyebrows.

"We're starving," announced Kit, who had been examining the beetles. "Is the bakery open?"

"Of course," said Pearl. She led the way through a narrow passageway, lined with yet more shelves packed with tins and parcels, and into the building next door. It had several ovens at one end and smelled pleasantly of baking. Pastries, loaves of bread and cakes were cooling on wire racks and were piled up on large plates. There was a long line of bulging brown paper bags, clearly containing yet more baked goods, packed up and ready for collection. The floor, like that of the shop, had a thin layer of sand scattered over it.

"Are there any shells today?" asked Kit, turning away from a tray of gingerbread biscuits that looked remarkably like starfish.

"I was just about to take them out," replied Pearl. She opened the door of the nearest oven and drew out a tray of pastries that were the size and shape of scallop shells. She tumbled them out onto a wire rack. Kit scooped up one in each hand and tossed one to Max.

"Be careful," she said. "They're hot."

Max bit into the pastry. It was the most delicious thing he'd ever tasted, and was definitely worth burning his tongue for. It was filled with a rich custard and the dough was sweet and flaky, but light as air.

"That's really good," he mumbled, his mouth full.

Pearl smiled. Max went to take another bite, then to his surprise, he saw that the pastry looked as if he hadn't touched it at all. Confused, he tore off another piece, but when he drew it away from his mouth, it still looked exactly the same.

"That's why I like them," said Kit, grinning at him.

"Try a sea urchin next," said Pearl.

Before Max could ask what it was, she'd placed a round little bun on a plate and pushed it towards him. He tried it. To begin with, he thought it tasted of strawberry, but then he thought it might be lemon. After yet another mouthful, he became convinced it was chocolate. Max examined the remaining piece, to see what on earth was actually in it, but it just looked like a plain white bun.

"How did you do that?" he asked, in amazement.

"I'm a sandwich," she said, smiling, then ambled off to attend to the ovens.

Max looked at Kit, who was tearing away at a scallop shell.

"What?" she said, catching sight of his expression.

"Pearl just said she was a sandwich," hissed Max, keeping his voice low so Pearl couldn't hear. "I mean, she obviously likes baking, but if she thinks that—"

"Sand witch," interrupted Kit, with a snort of laughter. "She said sand WITCH, not sandwich. Honestly."

"What's so funny?" asked Pearl, coming back over to them.

Kit stopped laughing so suddenly that she choked on her pastry.

"Is this a cafe as well?" asked Max. He desperately wanted to know what a sand witch was, but he didn't want Pearl to think they'd been laughing at her. She seemed so nice that he didn't want to upset her, whatever she was.

"No," said Pearl, sadly. "I've always wanted to open one, but I don't think I'd dare. It might upset Leandra. She's scared all the other shopkeepers into closing – she bullies everyone. The only reason I'm able to keep the shop going is because even Leandra realizes that the villagers need to get their food from somewhere. She's never picked on me yet. But she might if I did something as bold as open a cafe."

"Well you should," said Max. "I'd come along every day, if you did."

"Thank you," she said, with a smile.

"How much was that?" he asked, gesturing towards their plates.

"Nothing," she said, generously. "Since it's your first time in Yowling."

"Have you seen a kettle?" asked Kit, who had finally succeeded in polishing off one of the never-ending shell pastries. "A flying one, spinning around the place?"

"No," said Pearl, who didn't seem at all surprised by the question. "But I haven't left the shop."

"We should carry on looking," said Kit.

They said goodbye to Pearl and headed back through the shop next door.

"What's a sand witch?" asked Max, as soon as they were outside.

"She is," replied Kit simply. Then realizing that Max was expecting more, she gave a shrug.

"She's not a witch," she said. "Not in the way that you're thinking. A sand witch is a completely different thing – like the way that a seahorse is nothing to do with an actual horse. Sand witches can cast very weak charms, but only if they're near the sea. They're not really able to survive anywhere else – that's why she lives here."

"So that explains those scallop shells and sea urchins," said Max.

"The magic wears off as soon as you take them out of her shop, though," said Kit.

Max wished that Pearl would brave the Keeper and open a cafe. He wasn't looking forward to a summer of Bram's cooking.

Max and Kit spent ages searching the village for the runaway kettle. They knocked at doors, but hardly anyone answered. The ones who did only opened their doors a crack.

"They're scared of the Keeper," said Kit in explanation, as another door closed in their faces. "That's why everyone hides away."

Max got brief glimpses of the peculiar people inside, of green scaly skin, of claws instead of hands, of strange voices that rasped and creaked. But no one could help them. Yet even as they reached the seafront, Kit continued hunting.

"I'm sure we'll find it soon," she said, as she peered beneath the broken rowing boat.

Max found Kit's optimism hard to understand – privately, he was certain that it was a lost cause. He thought about the many disasters that could have befallen the kettle as he walked along the edge of the beach. He scuffled his shoes across the pebbles and shells, stopping every now and then to pick up a piece of jewel-coloured sea glass or to examine a strand of seaweed. Then he saw a pair of eyes, staring up at him from the sand.

"Urgh!" he cried, and leaped back.

A froglike face emerged, and then a man-sized chunk of the beach rose up as a person appeared. Max goggled at him in shock. The man – if you could call him that – had webbed scaly hands, bulbous yellow eyes and a large rubbery mouth, as if he was part human and part fish. He seemed to find Max every bit as peculiar, and was staring back at him with equal surprise.

"Hello, Tom," said Kit, coming over to join them.

"Yurp," said Tom, his eyes still fixed intently on Max.

"It's all right," said Kit. "He's related to Bram. This is his grandson."

"Ah," said Tom, blinking at last. "Welcome."

"Thanks," said Max, trying to keep his voice steady. "How did you…?" He gestured at the strip of beach from which Tom had appeared.

"Live there," said Tom.

"But how do you breathe under there?"

"Just do," said Tom flatly. Whatever Tom was, conversation did not seem to be his strong point.

"You haven't seen a kettle, have you?" asked Kit. "Spewing steam everywhere, whizzing about? A customer brought it in yesterday, but it got away before we could fix it."

"I have," said Tom slowly. "Reckoned it was something to do with you lot. It's safe."

He pointed a stubby webbed finger at the heap of lobster pots beside the pier.

"Trapped it in one of them."

"Tom, you're amazing!" cried Kit and she flung her arms around him.

Tom looked surprised, but rather pleased.

The three of them picked their way across the sand. Kit and Max were telling Tom about how they had lost

68

the kettle, their voices carrying through the still air. They had almost reached the pier when Tom froze, staring with his bulging yellow eyes.

"What is it?" asked Kit.

But Tom didn't reply. Instead he sank down into the sand, which swallowed him up as if it was a sinkhole.

"That was weird," said Max fervently. He prodded the spot where Tom had been with his foot, but there was no sign of him at all. "What is he? He definitely isn't human. And how come he can just vanish like that?"

Kit didn't reply. She had gone very tense and rigid, rather like Tom, except that she didn't have the same option of vanishing in quite such an effective way.

"Max," she hissed. "We've got to go."

"What? Aren't we going to get the kettle first?"

"Not now," she said. "Let's just turn around and go back the way we came."

She tugged at Max's sleeve, but he didn't budge. He had spotted something. A woman with long dark hair was leaning against one of the wooden posts that supported the pier, watching them with interest.

"Who's that?" said Max, but Kit looked as if she was about to be sick.

"It's the Keeper. Leandra."

Max stared. He couldn't help it – he'd heard so much about her that he'd imagined an impossibly terrifying monster. In reality, Leandra didn't look frightening at all. She was quite young and pretty, for a grown-up. She had a heart-shaped face, very big eyes and a cloud of black hair. The strangest thing about her was her clothes. She was dressed entirely in black, an elaborate confection of lace and ruffles that looked completely inappropriate for the seaside, teamed with a pair of heavy boots that were covered in sharp silver studs.

"Hello!" she called, in a clear voice, and beckoned at them to come over.

"Oh no," said Kit, looking around wildly, as if she was planning an escape route.

"We could just ignore her?" suggested Max.

"No! That would be worse. We'll have to go over there, now that she's seen us."

They walked towards the spot beneath the pier, Kit reluctantly, Max with more interest. At last he was going to meet the Keeper that everyone kept talking about.

Leandra was watching them lazily as they approached, still leaning against the pier. Kit and Max stopped a little way away from her, and suddenly Max began to feel nervous.

"What on earth have you been up to?" she asked and gave them a wide smile. Her teeth were very white and her dark eyes gleamed. "I heard you from miles away. Your voices carried all the way over to the castle."

There was a steely edge to her voice – enough to stop Max from saying anything in reply. Leandra examined her hands, seemingly fascinated by her own fingernails. They were painted silver, extremely long, and the ends had been filed to sharp points. They looked like talons.

"You should really be more careful," she said, at last. She pointed a finger at Max and with a shock he saw that a yellow flame was dancing at the end of her nail. He jumped backwards, and Leandra grinned, then blew the flame out, as easily as if it was a birthday candle. Max stared in shock. Kit didn't seem surprised. She was just watching Leandra dully, like a mouse trapped between the paws of a bored cat.

Then Leandra stepped towards them and tapped Kit on the nose with the same finger that had been alight just a moment before. Kit closed her eyes in despair.

"You're the spellstopper's assistant," Leandra said. "Of course."

Kit didn't say anything.

"And who are you?" she asked, turning to Max.

71

"I'm Max," he said.

"So, Max," she said, still smiling. "What are you doing in the village?"

"We're looking for a lost kettle," said Max, feeling as if he had to say something. "We're just going to get it, then we're leaving right away."

"A kettle?" repeated Leandra, looking faintly amused. "How on earth did you manage to lose that?"

"It's magic," said Max, who was starting to feel slightly befuddled. He wished he could get away from her – it almost felt as if she was bewitching him. "It escaped."

A flicker of interest crossed Leandra's face.

"Well, let's go and get it then," she said. "Quickly, the tide's coming in."

She linked her arm through Max's and began to walk briskly back towards the seafront. Kit trailed a few steps behind them, miserably.

"Are you going to spellstop this kettle?" Leandra asked Max. "Can I watch?"

Max was feeling very uncomfortable. He had no idea what Leandra was going to do, and her sharp nails were digging into his arm.

"I don't know how," he said, wishing that Kit would say something.

"That's a shame," said Leandra. "I'm extremely interested in spellstopping. I used to know Bram very well. Once upon a time he worked for me. He helped me to keep the castle under control."

She sighed, then looked very intently at Max.

"What I really need, Max, is for Bram to agree to help me again. It would make such a difference. Do you think you could persuade him?"

"Um…" said Max uncertainly, wishing that she would let go of his arm.

"Because if he won't agree, I'll have to *make* him agree."

Max's skin prickled. He understood Kit's reaction now. All he wanted to do was get as far away from Leandra as possible.

At last, they reached the lobster pots.

"Well?" Leandra demanded, looking from the pile to Max.

Max gazed at the enormous mound of lobster pots. They were wooden cages netted with rope, piled up so high that they teetered above his head. There had to be at least a hundred of them. Because the cages were made from such thick rope and were mostly covered in seaweed, it was quite hard to see inside. A black cast-iron kettle would be almost invisible.

"I'll check this side, you do the other," muttered Kit.

They went to opposite sides of the mound and started examining each of the cages in turn. Leandra was tapping her foot and Max could feel the irritation radiating off her as she watched them search.

"Haven't you found it yet?" she asked impatiently. "Since it's so important to Bram, I think you should let me return it to him. He might finally agree to help me then."

Max's heart was thudding in alarm now. He didn't know what to do. The last thing he wanted was to give the kettle to Leandra. But what would she do to them if they didn't? He tried to catch Kit's eye, to see if she had a plan, but she just stared back at him wide-eyed, looking as panicked as he was. Then Leandra gave a loud, impatient sigh.

"This is ridiculous," she said. "This is what I think of your stupid kettle."

She stabbed her finger in the direction of the lobster pots and with a huge *whoosh*, the entire stack burst into flames.

The netting on the cages frazzled at once and the wooden frames crackled as they burned to a crisp. Max and Kit staggered backwards, away from the heat of the fire, flinging their arms in front of their faces to shield themselves from the blaze. From somewhere close by, Max heard Leandra laughing as if she was overcome by how funny it all was. Her peals of laughter became the hooting call of an owl, which rang in his ears, then died away as Max and Kit were left alone with the towering flames.

6

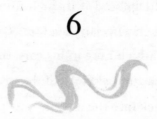

It was Tom who put the fire out – at least, it was thanks to Tom. As soon as the owl's cries faded away, Max and Kit saw him running towards them, his feet flapping, his eyes bulging even more than usual.

"My pots!" he cried, skidding to a halt beside them. They all looked helplessly up at the blazing fire. Max's face was flushed from the heat of it. The tide had crept further up the beach and waves were now lapping about the wooden posts of the pier.

Tom turned towards the sea and gave a strange trilling whistle. At once, a shape rose out of the waves. It was huge – the size of a house – and seemed to be made entirely of water. Max stared at it and thought he could make out a face – there were swirls of grey sea water forming two eyes and a mouth. Tom pointed frantically at the blazing fire. The thing gazed at the flames for a moment, then shot a great torrent of water out of its mouth, which cascaded over the flames like a waterfall. It splattered the ground with such force that Max was drenched through with salty sea spray. The fire went out, with a sizzling hiss.

Tom gave a funny sort of bow, and the shape disappeared back into the waves.

"What was that?" asked Kit. She was also soaked from head to toe and looked as puzzled as Max.

"Water spirit," said Tom, as if it was nothing out of the ordinary. He was already sifting through the charred mess of his lobster pots. Max was still staring at the spot where the thing had appeared, rendered temporarily speechless by how unbelievably strange it all was. Now he realized why Kit had advised against going swimming in the cove. She hadn't been exaggerating when she said it was full of magical monsters, even if this one had seemed quite helpful.

There was a sudden screeching noise as the kettle emerged from the charred heap, and tried to fly off. Kit leaped forwards, seized it firmly by the handle and stuffed it back into one of the few surviving lobster pots.

"Got it," she announced, triumphantly, as she slammed the little door of the lobster pot tightly shut.

Tom, meanwhile, had sat down miserably on the low sea wall and was making a faint moaning sound, as if he was suffering from a violent attack of indigestion.

"What's the matter?" asked Max.

"First my boat, now my pots," groaned Tom.

"Tom's a fisherman," said Kit. "If he's not able to work, half of Yowling will go hungry."

"What happened to your boat?" asked Max, looking over at the upturned vessel.

"Sea snake bit it," replied Tom gloomily.

"It can all be fixed," said Kit firmly. "I'll take some of the pots home today. I'll mend them for you. It's the least we can do. She'd have never set fire to them if we hadn't brought her over here."

Max felt a stab of guilt. He wished he hadn't said anything to Leandra. It was his fault really.

"Much obliged," said Tom, although he still looked woeful.

"Let's go back to my house," said Kit, and shoved two of the pots into Max's arms, before grabbing two for herself. "It's just up there."

She pointed at one of the steep narrow roads that led off the seafront.

"Shouldn't we get the kettle back to Bram?" asked

Max, nodding towards one of the lobster pots that Kit was holding, where the kettle sat imprisoned amongst a singed tangle of rope and seaweed, a miserable curl of steam coming out of its spout.

"An hour won't make any difference. It's safe now – that's the important thing. It'll only take Bram a minute to fix it – there'll still be loads of time before the customer comes back to collect it this evening."

"Okay," said Max, secretly glad that they weren't going back to Bram's just yet. Even though his clothes were unpleasantly damp, he was curious to see what Kit's house was like.

They said goodbye to Tom and set off. Tom gave a glum nod in return and continued to stare miserably at the burned heap of wood and netting.

"Next time you see Leandra, don't hang around," advised Kit, as they climbed up some rocky steps. "Otherwise things like this happen."

"She's terrifying," said Max fervently. "I thought she seemed okay at first, until…"

"Yeah," said Kit. "Like I said before, that's why everyone in Yowling hides away so much. If they don't, it's only a matter of time before Leandra does something to them."

"But why, though?" asked Max. "Why is she so horrible to everyone?"

"I think she's bored," replied Kit. "She's not like the rest of us – she's bound to the castle so she can't ever leave. I think she takes it out on the village. She's angry, so she bullies everyone."

Max fell silent. He was beginning to realize why his mother had been so keen to keep him away from Yowling. It was a far more dangerous place than he'd originally thought.

They turned down yet another twisty side street, where the houses were even more irregular and jumbled together than the ones Max had seen previously. He glanced into the nearest window and saw a black cat sitting on the sill, staring intently at him with big green eyes.

"This is where I live," said Kit, as they reached the most peculiar house of all. The front of it was entirely covered with a thick leafy creeper, which obscured most of the windows. There didn't seem to be a way in, but Kit pushed back a curtain of the climbing plant to reveal a red front door.

"You live here?" said Max, astonished. Kit just grinned.

"My mother likes gardening," she said, as she opened the door and went in.

Max followed her, and the curtain of climbers swished back into place behind them. Inside were more plants. There were pots of earth lined up along the sides of the dark hallway, filled with seedlings sprouting little green shoots.

They left the damaged lobster pots and the still-steaming kettle just inside the front door, then Max went over to have a better look at the plants.

"Careful," warned Kit. "They're delicate."

"I know about plants," said Max confidently.

They'd made a garden at his school and he'd tended to all sorts of vegetables, from pink and white radishes to climbing runner beans. He squatted down on the ground and touched one of the little seedlings. Instantly, it shrivelled up and died.

"Told you," said Kit, then broke off as a woman came down the stairs.

She had the same auburn hair as Kit and wore a gardener's apron that was covered in dirt. She carried a pair of secateurs in one hand and a bundle of branches in the other. Max got to his feet guiltily, hoping she wouldn't notice the dead seedling.

"I was trimming the plumdrum tree," she said, by way of explanation. "The only way of reaching the top is by hanging out of the upstairs windows."

There was a series of loud thumps and a little girl of about six tore downstairs, then stopped abruptly when she saw Max.

"That's my sister, Eppie," said Kit.

"Why are you so wet?" asked Eppie, staring suspiciously at Max.

"That's exactly what I was going to ask," said Kit's mother. "What happened?"

She looked shaken, if not exactly surprised, when they told her, then she bundled them upstairs to change their clothes. Kit insisted on dragging the lobster pots with her, and Max was surprised to see that her bedroom resembled a workshop. There were all sorts of carpentry tools and even a set of soldering irons.

"Did you make those things?" he asked, his eyes drawn to a collection of wooden boxes, spinning tops and skittles lined up on the bedroom shelves.

Kit nodded.

"I've always loved making and repairing stuff," she said. "I've never wanted to do anything else. That's why I was so keen to be Bram's assistant."

"Don't you go to school?"

"School?" said Kit blankly. "What's that?"

"You don't know what school is?" asked Max, unable to believe what he was hearing. "You go there to learn stuff."

"What sort of things?" asked Kit, sounding interested.

"Maths and English, mainly. And PE, which is mostly just running around after a ball."

"Oh." Kit's face fell. "I thought it might be something to do with learning about magic."

Max was beginning to realize just how cut off Yowling was from the outside world. It was like being on another planet. He refused Kit's offer of a spare boiler suit, and instead found himself in a large fisherman's jersey that belonged to Kit's father. It was far too big for him, but he rolled the sleeves up. He kept his own trousers.

They went downstairs and out into the little courtyard garden, and Kit's mother brought them some lemonade. The garden was surrounded by four high walls and there was barely room for a table and chairs, but what it lacked in space, it made up for by the sheer volume of green. They sat in the dappled shade of the newly trimmed plumdrum tree, which had dark purple leaves and bright red fruits that looked like strawberries. Each of the walls was completely covered in leafy climbers and every single windowsill was crammed with containers that brimmed with strange plants. Max stared at the nearest one, fascinated. It was full of thick fleshy flowers, which looked a bit like petunias, but they constantly changed colour – blue, purple, red, orange and yellow – so that a whole rainbow unfolded as he watched them.

"They're called chromacups," said Kit. "You get used to them after a while. Although Mum's always finding something new. She's got plants in literally every room in the house. When I was younger, I almost got eaten by a Venezuelan shark fern. Since then she's mostly stuck to non-lethal varieties."

"What does she do with them all?" asked Max, thinking of the rows of seedlings in the hall. "Surely there's not enough space in here."

"She sells them. By mail order, usually. She'd really like to open a plant nursery here but she knows it would be a bad idea."

"Why?" said Max, not thinking.

Kit raised her eyebrows.

"Why do you think?" she asked, and Max understood. Leandra.

Max felt something tickling his ankle and, looking

down, he saw that the thick mat under his feet was alive. Little tendrils were waving up at him, and knotting themselves into his shoelaces. He lifted up his foot and they sprang back at once. Max set his foot back down on the ground again, very gently so as not to hurt them.

"It's only the seedlings you have to worry about," said Kit, who seemed amused by how careful he was being. "The bigger plants are tough enough to look after themselves. See?"

She grabbed hold of a branch of the plumdrum tree, pulled off one of the knobbly red fruits, and popped it into her mouth.

Max was still fascinated by the thick living carpet that was twisting and waving beneath his feet. It was studded with thousands of tiny blue flowers. He leaned down to touch one. As soon as he did, he felt a familiar pain, as if he'd been snapped with an elastic band. The flower withered. What was worse was that it wasn't just the one flower. The entire plant shrivelled and died so that the whole floor of the courtyard turned a dark, dead brown. Max was horrified.

"Oh," said Kit, equally shocked.

"What's happened?" Kit's mother appeared in the doorway, holding a fresh jug of lemonade, and looked across the dead courtyard with dismay.

"I'm so sorry," said Max. "I just touched it. I didn't do anything else, I promise."

"It's fine," she said, although she seemed a bit taken aback. "I can easily grow another one."

But the more that Kit and her mother told Max not to worry about it, the more Max did. It was like his problems with electricity, all over again. Maybe it was getting worse now he was surrounded by magical things? Maybe, at the rate he was going, he'd end up hurting people as well? It was too awful a thought to contemplate. He had a sudden overwhelming urge to go back home to London, so that he could shut himself away in his little bedroom. A horrible feeling of homesickness hit him, and he tried not to let his voice wobble when he next spoke.

"I think I'll go home," he said. "To Bram's, I mean."

"I'll come with you," said Kit, at once.

"No," said Max. "It's okay, I can remember the way back."

He saw Kit give her mother a quick look, and felt even more like an outsider.

"Are you sure?" she said and Max nodded.

Kit went with him to the front door.

"It was just an accident," she said. "It's fine – Mum can grow another one."

Max just nodded miserably.

"Here," she said, handing him a bag that was knotted tightly at the top. "I put the kettle in there. At least Bram'll be happy we found it. I'll be over again tomorrow, unless he needs me this afternoon."

"Tell your mum I really am sorry," said Max again. He rolled down the sleeves of the oversized jumper and pulled the rollneck up about his face, so there was no chance he'd accidentally brush against the climbers that hung in front of the door on his way out. The last thing he needed was to kill something else. He'd hoped that coming to Yowling would mean that he'd get rid of his problem. Instead it just seemed to be getting worse.

7

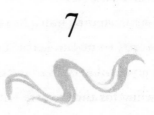

Bram seemed to know that something was up as soon as Max arrived back at the farmhouse. After congratulating him for finding the kettle, Bram made them both a mug of tea and listened as Max told him what had happened on the beach.

The moment Max mentioned Leandra's name, Bram almost leaped out of his seat. Tea sloshed all over the table, but Bram didn't seem to notice.

"What did she do?" he croaked. "She didn't hurt you, did she?"

"She set fire to some lobster pots," admitted Max.

"You've GOT to stay away from her. Did she guess that we were related?"

"I think so," said Max uncertainly.

"Course she did," muttered Bram, more to himself than to Max. "She'd have seen you yesterday in the van, wouldn't she? She was flying right alongside the window."

"Why won't you help her with the castle?" asked Max. "Kit said you've fixed it before."

"Because that woman is evil," said Bram firmly. "I reckon the only way to stop her is to leave the castle be. Hopefully it'll go down and take her with it. She's been terrorizing Yowling for thirty years – it's time someone stood up to her."

"Thirty years?" Max frowned. Leandra didn't look that old.

"Yep. She just appeared one day, replaced the old Keeper. Been a nightmare ever since. The last one was bad enough, but at least he didn't have flames coming out of his fingers.

"The Keepers have a different sort of lifespan to us," continued Bram. "It's something to do with living in the castle. They always stay the same age. You never see them as children and they never get older. I reckon they spend their early lives as birds. And when a new one is ready to take over, the old one goes – turns back into an owl."

"How long have they owned the castle?"

"They're not the owners – they've always just looked after it. They were little more than housekeepers to start with. No, the castle was made by a sorcerer."

"A sorcerer?" The word felt strange on Max's tongue. He must have sounded as if he didn't believe it, because Bram frowned.

"Yes, a sorcerer. Where do you think all the magical things we spellstop come from? The only people who can create things like that are sorcerers, but you'll likely never meet one. You think spellstoppers are rare? Sorcerers are rarer still. You might only get one in a hundred years, if that."

Bram rubbed his eyes wearily, before continuing.

"So, a sorcerer built Yowling Castle then left it in the care of the Keepers. But I don't think they ever intended to leave it for so long. So now the magic's going bad. It started happening before Leandra's time, but it's been getting worse. Reckon that's why she's been getting worse too – the Keepers and the castle are both so bound together. She shouldn't be able to set fire to things like that."

"Why don't you spellstop the castle then?" asked Max. "Take all of the magic away from it, I mean, instead of just fixing it?"

"Too big a job. There's never been a spellstopper alive who'd be capable of that. It takes a lot more out of you, eliminating magic completely. The truth is, Max, I'm not even able to fix it. Last time I worked on the castle, the effort nearly killed me. And it's worse now. Leandra's just trying to force me into doing something that I'm not able to do. It's better for everyone – not just me, but everyone in Yowling, too – if I don't help her. I'll just mind my own business and stick to mending antiques – it's much simpler."

"What about the village?" asked Max.

"If the castle goes down? Don't think it'll have any effect on it. No matter how bad that castle gets, there's no sign of anything going physically wrong in Yowling. They're not connected in any magical way, no matter what Leandra thinks. No, the village will be better off without the castle – and the Keepers."

Bram sank back into his chair and fell silent. Max felt even more worried than before. Everything suddenly seemed very serious. Not only was the situation with the castle far worse than he had imagined, but his own problems were getting worse too, since he'd now progressed to killing things with a single touch.

"Is something the matter?" asked Bram, noticing the worried expression on Max's face. "I shouldn't have let you go into Yowling – you don't need to be caught up in all of this."

"It's not that," said Max miserably, and he told Bram about killing the plants at Kit's house. To his surprise, Bram seemed utterly unconcerned.

"That's exactly what you'd expect from an untrained spellstopper," he said, cheering up, as if Max had just told him some excellent news.

"But if I kill magical plants, does that mean I could kill magical people?" asked Max, who was not feeling at all comforted. Somehow, killing the plants had shaken him more than anything else that had happened so far.

"No!" said Bram firmly. "People are completely different. If someone's born with something magical about them, you can't interfere with that."

"You said you'd teach me how to control this thing I have."

"And I'm going to," said Bram. "Bring me that kettle – we'll start right now."

Max went over to the back door, picked up the bag from where he'd left it, and brought it over to the table.

"Just set it down in the middle," instructed Bram. He unknotted the bag and the kettle rolled out. It was covered in soot and looked a little battered after its adventure, but it still gave an angry whistle when it spotted Bram and Max.

"So, the trick is to empty your mind," said Bram, picking it up. "Think of lightning conductors – those metal rods that run down the side of tall buildings. The charge passes through them without damaging them. It's the same idea."

The kettle began to glow, as if it was very hot, but Bram kept talking.

"Once you've cleared your mind, you can start feeling the energy that's coming from an object," he said. "You can feel if it's imbalanced. It'll want to return to its original state, the state it was in when it was first enchanted. So you need to let that excess energy flow through you, and release it – either into the ground or into the air. I prefer the ground, but it's up to you. Every spellstopper has their own technique."

The kettle faded back to its original colour. Bram was silent for a moment, as he examined it.

"There," he said with satisfaction, and he handed it to Max. "Done."

Max lifted the lid and peered inside. It looked just like an ordinary cast iron kettle.

"Try tipping it into your mug," suggested Bram.

Max replaced the lid, picked it up and tilted it above his empty mug. At once, a stream of thick hot chocolate poured out of the spout and filled his mug to the brim.

"No way," said Max in disbelief. He put down the kettle, picked up his mug and took a tentative sip. It tasted rich and creamy, like the perfect hot chocolate. It was incredible.

"That's what it was supposed to do all along," said Bram, who was grinning from ear to ear. "Whatever you most want to drink, it should pour it for you. Coffee, lemonade, whisky…whatever you like."

"Wow," said Max, deeply impressed. "Do we have to give it back?"

"'Fraid so," said Bram. "That's how I make a living, fixing things like these. Enchanted objects are very rare, but they're so prized that people will travel from all over the world just to get them repaired."

He got to his feet and disappeared for a moment. Max was still intrigued by the kettle. He had just got a glass to see if it really would pour out whisky, when Bram returned, carrying a large cardboard box in his arms.

"No point starting you on spellstopping till you've got a handle on electricity," he said. "Magic's a stronger form of energy, so you'll have to get over the electricity thing first – that's why you've been having problems with it. The two are linked, see? Anyway, I had a hunt around the house earlier and found some old things that use electricity for you to practise on."

Max peered into the box. It was crammed with all sorts of objects that he would never have imagined Bram possessing, from hairdryers and curling tongs to children's toys.

"They're mostly your mother's, from when she was younger," said Bram, by way of explanation. "Or your grandmother's."

Max knew that his grandmother – Bram's wife – had died before he was born, but he still found it quite odd, seeing so many things from the past. It made him realize that Bram used to have a completely different sort of life, one in which the farmhouse had been filled with his family.

Max fished out a portable radio from amongst the clutter and turned it around in his hands, examining it.

"You need to keep yourself calm, if you want to turn it on without breaking it," said Bram. "Personally, I always find that it's worse when I'm feeling out of sorts – once I empty my mind a bit, I'm fine. It's exactly the same principle as spellstopping, except that magical objects are a lot more sensitive."

Max took a deep breath, preparing himself. Much as he hated to admit it, he was nervous. Years of getting a shock every time he touched something electrical made his whole body tense up in anticipation. He told himself sternly to relax, then flicked the switch to turn the power on. There was a loud pop as the radio broke, and Max felt a stab of pain in his hand. His heart sank.

"Never mind," said Bram, with a shrug. He began to pull on his boots, getting ready to go back out into the workshop. "Just keep on trying – you'll get there in the end."

It took Max almost a week before he got the hang of it. He ended up breaking every single item that Bram had given him, but finally he was able to switch on his bedroom light using his bare hands, something he hadn't been able to do for years. He'd even managed to call his mother from the ancient telephone that lived in the hallway. It had been the best feeling in the world to hear her answer the phone and yell with joy when she realized that he'd been able to call her, all by himself. Granted, he'd lost concentration and the telephone had short-circuited shortly afterwards, but still. He was definitely getting better.

When he wasn't practising, he spent his time in the workshop, watching Bram and Kit as they worked on a collection of unusual objects. Max's favourite part was getting to see the customers. There was a steady stream of them. Some of them came by car or van, others arrived on foot, and one had even landed a helicopter in the field behind the house, which had terrified the dogs and blown a couple of tiles off the roof. Some of the customers looked quite ordinary. They arrived in jeans and T-shirts, or in blazers and shirts and neatly pressed trousers, and would often look rather embarrassed at the prospect of explaining why they were there. These were the humans, many of whom had inherited pieces from more magical relatives without fully realizing what they had taken on.

Others were clearly from the magical community. Most of these people had something subtly different about them, like the mysteriously bandaged owner of the kettle. Even if they looked completely human, Max soon instinctively knew if they weren't. The magical beings all had a different atmosphere about them, as if they were slightly wider awake than other people. They also seemed more at ease in the farmyard – or perhaps that was because the dogs tended to leave them alone after their initial volley of barks. Whenever a regular human arrived,

Banana and Sardine would howl constantly, while Treacle would simply stare at the unfortunate visitor while emitting a constant, threatening growl.

As the weeks passed, the stock in Bram's workshop slowly renewed itself. The cannon was collected by a nervous man in a dark suit, who drove his car into the yard and was so terrified of the dogs that he refused to get out. Instead, they handed him the cannon through the window and he gave them an envelope of cash in return.

A china doll who had developed an unpleasant habit of being sick over anyone who touched her had been carefully restored and returned to a plump woman in a handknitted jumper, who had bright violet eyes and seemed delighted that her family heirloom had returned to singing Scottish airs instead of retching constantly. In their places were a portrait of a stern Victorian gentleman who hypnotized anyone who looked at him for too long, an enchanted music box with a broken lid for Kit to repair, and a sapphire ring that was supposed to bring good fortune to whoever wore it, but had instead started to squeeze the wearer's finger so tightly that it would go blue and bloodless and almost drop off before the ring would release its grip.

At first, Max was content to watch and learn, but now he was eager to join in. He was tired of doing all the boring jobs, like sweeping the floor or sorting out boxes of nails and screws.

"Can't I help with something?" he begged, when Bram seemed to be in a particularly mellow mood. "What about the ring? You said you weren't looking forward to doing that one."

"That's because it's vicious," retorted Bram. "I wouldn't let you near it unless you were far more experienced."

"Isn't there anything I can practise on?" asked Max.

"What about the weasel?" suggested Kit, looking up from polishing a chair leg with beeswax. "That's been sitting around for ages."

"I'd forgotten about the weasel!" exclaimed Bram. "Kit, that's an excellent idea."

He went over to the shelf and picked up the stuffed weasel that Max had noticed the first time he had been in Bram's workshop.

"Found it in the yard, years ago," said Bram. "Whoever left it there must have wanted to get rid of it – it's been here ever since."

Max could see why it had been abandoned. The

weasel was standing on a wooden plinth, clutching a log between its paws. Its teeth were bared, its fur was balding and falling away in patches, and something about the knuckles of its claws looked uncomfortably human.

As Bram brought it over to the workbench, holding it by the very edges of its stand, the weasel ground its jaws and made a dusty gurgling sound.

"All it does is try to bite you," said Bram cheerfully. "It's got no magical powers apart from that. I left it as it was because I thought it had a bit more character this way. But it'll be good for you to practise on."

Max moved towards it, but Bram stopped him.

"Try taking off your shoes first," he advised. "That can help when you're learning. Makes it easier for the magic to drain away, if you're not used to it."

Max kicked off his runners and stood there in his socks.

"Remember what I told you before," said Bram. "Once you're calm and your mind's empty, you'll start to feel the energy that's coming off it. You want that excess energy to run out of it into you, and then you let it drain away. Don't get distracted midway through – it'll be like getting electrocuted and the magic will just shoot back into the object again. If you touch it and feel that the energy's too much, just keep your mind blank, and break your connection. That way, you won't get hurt."

Max nodded. Kit had stopped her polishing and was sitting in the armchair, watching him with interest.

He slowly reached out a hand, and the weasel immediately snaked forwards and bit him.

"Ow!" yelled Max, rubbing his thumb. A trickle of blood oozed down it.

Bram rummaged around for a plaster.

"Here you go," he said, handing a crumpled packet to Max.

"Thanks," said Max, and wrapped one around his thumb.

He took a few deep breaths, trying to clear his mind again.

The weasel looked at him beadily, still gnashing its teeth. Its paws flexed on its log, as if it was getting ready to spring.

"It's stuck on, isn't it?" asked Max, peering at the underside of the weasel. "I mean, it can't jump at me?"

"Nope," said Bram, prodding it. "Glued down."

"Good," said Max, and reached out again, more gingerly this time.

He decided to go for the top of the creature's head –

at least that way it wouldn't be able to bite him.

As soon as he touched it, he felt a surge running through him. So this was magic. It felt like electricity – a crackling, jolting, powerful surge that shocked through him. He jerked his hand away at once and reeled back, feeling as if he'd just been punched in the stomach. The weasel cackled at him wheezily, clicking its teeth together.

"Are you okay?" said Kit, in concern.

"Take a minute," said Bram gently. "Go outside, get some air."

"Let me have another try," insisted Max. The pain had subsided a little, but he still felt a numb, tingling feeling in his hands and feet. "I know what to expect this time."

He closed his eyes for a few seconds, trying to steady his thoughts, then he approached the stuffed weasel for the third time, padding towards it in his thin socks. The weasel swiped at him with its claws. It seemed more alert than before, as if its encounters with Max had woken it up, and it chattered at him angrily.

Max spun the plinth around, and grabbed hold of the weasel's back. As soon as his hands made contact with the rough fur, the energy hit him once more. He tried to do as Bram had said, to channel it down through him, and let it drain away. But it was impossible. Pain shot through him, forcing him to cry out.

"Let go of it!" yelled Bram.

But Max would not let go. Bram grabbed his wrist, pulling him away, and at once the stabbing feeling stopped.

"Don't fight it," said Bram seriously. "Just keep your mind calm."

"I was calm!" protested Max. He felt angry, as if he wanted to lash out at something in frustration. He kicked at the workbench, forgetting that he had no shoes on.

"Ow!" he yelled, as he stubbed his toe. It felt as if everything was against him. He was beginning to think that he'd never learn how to spellstop. A part of him had thought that once he'd cracked it, he might be able to help Bram – that together they might be able to do something to stop Leandra. But it was no use. Perhaps Bram was wrong to believe in him so much. Maybe he didn't have it in him to be a spellstopper after all.

"You've had enough for one day," said Bram firmly, interrupting Max's gloomy thoughts. "Both of you, get out of here. Do something else. I heard the ice-cream van's in Yowling today. Go down and buy one – just make sure to keep yourselves safe."

He drew a crumpled ten-pound note from his pocket and gave it to Kit, while Max put his shoes back on.

"Don't worry about spellstopping," he said to Max, clapping him on the shoulder. "You've only just started. You'll get there."

Max didn't feel quite so optimistic.

8

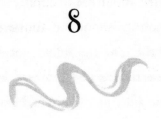

You would not have known that there was an ice-cream van on the beach unless somebody pointed it out to you. It had parked in the most out of the way spot, right in the crook of the cliffs at the edge of the village. The van itself had been camouflaged – a thick sheet, the colour of sand, had been pegged over it, like a large tent, with bits of seaweed and marram grass stuck to it. As Max and Kit approached, they saw Pearl emerge from underneath the tented edge, peer around, then scuttle off back towards the village, holding an ice-cream cone out carefully in front of her, as if she was doing some sort of strange egg and spoon race.

"Why—" began Max, but Kit cut him off with just one word.

"Leandra."

They picked their way across the sandy path, shells

crunching underfoot, the tang of sea salt in the air. Max saw that because of the way that the cliffs jutted out, you couldn't see the castle from this inlet, which meant that it was a safe haven from the watchful eyes of the Keeper. They reached the tent and finally got a proper look at the van that was hidden inside. It was dark green, with a counter on the side, just like you'd expect. A cheerful man with dark hair and eyes stood behind the counter, wearing a green apron and a stripy shirt.

"Hello, Kit," he said. "Who's your friend?"

"This is Max," said Kit. "Max, meet Omar. Wait till you try his ice cream. He's a genius."

"No," protested Omar modestly. "Not a genius. I'm just good at figuring out what people like."

Max was peering to see what sort of ice cream Omar sold, but there wasn't anything on display, not even a list of flavours.

Omar looked intently at Max for a moment, then pulled out a cone that was the colour of milk chocolate. Then he scraped up three fat curls of ice cream and plopped them into it, one on top of the other.

"Try this," he said, handing it to Max. "I have a feeling you'll like it." Then he set about making another ice cream for Kit.

106

"That looks quite chocolatey," said Kit, looking at Max's ice cream with faint dislike.

"I know," said Max, pleased. He took an experimental lick. The top scoop was the creamiest chocolatiest ice cream he had ever tasted, studded with little chunks of white chocolate. The middle layer was a sort of butterscotch, which was fudgy and sweet, flecked with flakes of crunchy sea salt. The bottom layer was like the base of a cheesecake, but in ice-cream form. It was biscuity and rich, with a malty flavour, and the cone itself was made from crackly chocolate wafer. If somebody had asked Max to describe his perfect ice cream, it would have been this one.

He was momentarily distracted by the arrival of Kit's cone, which looked completely different.

"What's in yours?" Max asked, as she tucked in.

"Raspberry and pomegranate, honeycomb and clotted cream, with a ginger snap cone," said Omar, smiling.

Max, who hated ginger, thought that sounded terrible. Kit, though, seemed very happy.

Two more customers came into the tent – a tall blond man in a navy-blue fisherman's jersey, holding the hand of a small, equally blonde girl.

Max recognized the girl at once. It was Eppie. He also recognized the jumper – it was the same one that Kit's mother had lent him.

"Hello, Kit," said the man, looking surprised. "I'd have bought you an ice cream if I'd known you were coming down here."

"This is my dad," said Kit proudly. "Dad, this is Max."

"I've heard a lot about you," said the man. "I thought you two were working."

"We've got the rest of the day off," said Kit and Max felt a sudden stab of shame. It reminded him of how bad he was at spellstopping.

"In that case, would you mind taking Eppie home?" asked Kit's father. "That way, I can go for a swim."

"Can't I come?" asked Eppie, her face falling.

"Another time," said her father kindly, passing her an ice-cream cone – a toffee, rice puff and jelly baby confection, covered with multicoloured sugar sprinkles. Then he said goodbye to them and headed towards the sea.

Max watched, intrigued and a little surprised, as he strode into the water fully clothed, ducked underneath the waves and vanished from sight. He kept expecting to see Kit's dad surface again, but he didn't. It was the strangest thing. He turned to Kit, about to ask her about it, but saw that she was squinting up into the sky, frowning. Max followed her gaze and saw that a bird was flying towards them.

"What's the matter?" he began, then broke off as a shadow swooped across them, blocking out the bright sunlight. A second bird had swept past, high above their heads. Max saw that there were even more of them, gliding over the waves from the castle, heading straight for them.

"We need to leave now!" Kit's ice cream fell onto the sand. She didn't even seem to realize she'd dropped it, but seized Eppie by the hand and started to run, away from the owls and the village, towards the high cliffs.

For a second, Max froze. Then he spotted a familiar figure, striding across the beach in her heavy clumpy boots, her black dress and dark hair swirling about her. Leandra had arrived and she was looking right at him.

"Get out of here!" Omar shouted to Max. "You're in danger – don't you understand? The owls always bring trouble! Run!"

Max's legs finally came unstuck. The last thing he wanted was to be responsible for something else being burned to a crisp. The remnants of his ice-cream cone fell from his fingers as he tore after Kit, racing towards the cliffs as fast as he could. But although Max was running at full speed, several of the owls were following him. He could hear the swoosh of their wings as they hovered just above him, keeping pace almost lazily. The rough grey rocks of the cliffs loomed up ahead and he skidded to a halt, wondering where to go next. Kit and Eppie had vanished. A pair of sharp talons scraped the top of his scalp, and he fell to his knees, trying to beat off the creatures.

"In here!"

Kit was peering out at him from behind a fold in the cliff face. Max scrambled forwards, stumbling towards her. She dragged him behind the rock, into the narrowest of gullies.

"Quick, down here," said Kit, and she pointed to a crack in the cliff – a thin triangular gap that looked like the sort of hole that an animal might live in. Max scrambled inside and found himself in a narrow tunnel that had been hewn through the ancient limestone. It was very dark and wet. He could still hear the owls' haunting cries as they circled above the cliffs, searching for him.

"That was close," said Kit, as she squeezed into the

tunnel after him. "It's almost like they're following you, Max."

"I hope not," he retorted, then looked around and realized that Kit's sister was nowhere to be seen. "Where's Eppie? Is she okay?"

"She's fine," said Kit. "What about you – are you all right?"

"Yeah," said Max, rubbing his head. He could still feel the place where the owl's talons had brushed him, but it didn't seem to have broken the skin. "What was all that about?"

"I dunno," said Kit, frowning. "It was weird that they arrived so soon after we did. I hope she isn't trailing you – if she's worked out that you're Bram's grandson, maybe she thinks she can use you somehow, to force Bram to fix the castle."

Max was still trying to catch his breath after his frantic sprint across the sands. He felt shocked by what had just happened. Although he'd already been aware that Leandra was dangerous, he hadn't realized that the rest of the owls might attack too. He hoped fervently that Omar was all right. But if Kit was correct, it was Max that they were after.

"I think we'd better hide in here until things have

settled down," said Kit. "It's too risky to go back outside right now. Come on – Eppie will be wondering what's happened to us."

She turned and started to crawl along the tunnel and Max followed, as they went through the dripping wet rock towards the heart of the cliffs. It felt oppressive, as if the mass of stone was pressing down on him and could collapse at any moment.

"Where are we going?" he asked, struggling to see in the dim light.

"Wait and see," said Kit, without turning round. "Careful with this bit."

She slid away from him, out of sight. Max felt the tunnel slope sharply downwards. He lost his balance and fell, landing hard on his elbows, just beside Kit. As he scrambled to his feet, he gasped in wonder.

They had come out into a huge underground grotto. Shafts of light filtered through cracks in the roof, and it had the quiet, solemn feeling of a church. But that wasn't the most curious thing about the space. Every inch of its surface was covered in shells, which had been arranged into intricate patterns. There were swirls and stars and flowers and arches, picked out in shells of all shapes and sizes. Max was surprised at how many colours there were

– yellows and pinks and whites, blue crescents of mussel shells and dark grey oblongs of razor clams. There were thousands of shells, maybe even millions. They covered the ceiling, the walls and the floor under their feet. There was only one place that wasn't studded with shells and that was the large round pool that was sunk into the centre of the grotto, the water black and still. Eppie was skipping around the edge of the pool, singing to herself. It had the strangest atmosphere of anywhere he'd ever been – it almost felt like it had an energy all of its own.

"This is incredible," said Max, running his hand along the walls, his fingers bumping along the uneven surface of the shellwork.

"Weird, isn't it?" said Kit, grinning at the surprise on Max's face. "I found this place completely by accident. I've no idea what it was built for – I don't know if anyone else even knows it's here."

"And you can only get to it through that gap in the rock?" said Max.

"That's the only way in," said Kit. "You've got to wonder why anyone would go to so much trouble."

There was a sudden scream as Eppie lost her balance on the slippery surface and fell into the deep pool with a tremendous splash. She was swallowed up by the inky black water at once.

"Eppie!" yelled Kit in alarm. She looked at the pool in horror, then took a deep breath and jumped in after her sister. She, too, sank immediately.

Max stared at the spot where they had been, waiting for them to break the surface of the water. But they didn't. Heart thudding, he kicked off his shoes and was about to dive in after them, when Kit broke through the surface of the water, and was propelled towards the edge of the pool by a small sleek creature, with whiskers and white fur. It was a young seal. The seal pushed Kit towards the edge, and Kit grasped hold of the shell-covered side, choking. Max grabbed her arm and helped her up. The seal bobbed under the water and re-emerged as Eppie, who clambered out too.

"You shouldn't have gone in after me," protested Eppie.

Kit was doubled over, gasping for breath and coughing up water.

"She's not very good at swimming," said Eppie to Max.

"I thought you were in trouble," spluttered Kit. "You screamed."

"I was surprised! It wasn't like I meant to fall in."

"You turned into a seal," said Max faintly. Although Kit had told him about her family, and he'd seen her father disappear into the sea, it was still a shock seeing Eppie transform like that.

"Of course I did," said Eppie proudly. "It's easy."

"She's been like this since she was a toddler," said Kit, wringing water out of her hair.

Eppie was beaming. "I'll be able to go out to sea properly soon," she announced. "Dad said he'd take me."

Kit looked a bit downcast at this, and Max felt sorry for her.

"Do you want my jumper?" he offered. "You must be cold."

"No, I'm okay," said Kit. "Eppie, are you warm enough?"

"I don't feel the cold," boasted Eppie, skipping around the edge of the pool again. "I'm imperious."

"She means impervious," said Kit. "She's right though. Selkies don't really get wet like humans – they repel water."

Sure enough, Eppie's hair was already dry, while Kit's was still soaking wet.

"Why can't you transform?" asked Max curiously. "If Eppie and your father can?"

"They thought I was going to," she said, looking miserable. "Apparently I transformed once or twice, when I was really young. But then it just sort of stopped happening. Mum said I almost drowned when I was little, so maybe that had something to do with it."

Kit stared into the pool, unhappily.

"And now, I'm not even a good swimmer," she said. "It seems so unfair. Everyone I know has got some magical ability, except me."

"I don't," said Max, and Kit gave him a funny look.

"Of course you do!" she cried. "Why else would you have so many problems with electricity? You're a born spellstopper."

"You fix magical things too," said Max, who felt bad for Kit.

"Not properly. I just do the practical stuff, not the magical bits."

"Well Bram seems pretty impressed. He's always going on about how much he depends on you."

"Really?" said Kit, sounding a bit more cheerful, even though her teeth were chattering in the chilly air of the cave.

"Let's go back so you can warm up," suggested Max. "Surely the owls will have gone by now?"

"All right," agreed Kit. "You should tell Bram what happened though. If Leandra's following you, he should know about it."

They retrieved Eppie, then crawled back through the hole in the rock. Much as Max disliked the narrow, stifling tunnel, he was feeling even more uneasy about leaving it. If the owls really were watching out for him, then he wasn't safe anywhere.

9

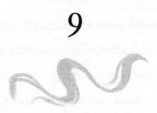

There was no sign of the owls, but something bad had clearly happened. The entire stretch of beach was deserted – there was only the odd ice-cream cone, squashed into the sand, to suggest that anyone had been there at all. A curl of foul-smelling smoke drifted into the air nearby and Max saw that there was just a blackened, charred lump where the ice-cream van had once stood.

"Oh!" said Kit, her face falling as she surveyed the scene.

Eppie, who was just behind her, burst into tears.

Max sprinted towards the van, praying that Omar wasn't still in it. The van had been tipped onto its side, its wheels in the air, and was now just a blackened, burned-out shell. Pieces of shredded tarpaulin floated about the beach, scattered by the breeze.

He peered through the van's shattered windows, feeling sick with apprehension.

"I escaped, at least," said a voice.

Omar came around the side of the van. His neat apron and striped shirt were streaked with ash, and he held a metal ice-cream scoop in one hand.

"It's the only thing I could salvage," he said, showing it to Max. "Leandra burned everything else."

"I'm so sorry," said Max, feeling terrible for him.

"Why would she do something like this?" burst out Omar. "I've never done anything to offend her!"

"Maybe we could all get together and stand up to her," suggested Max. It seemed unbelievable that Leandra was able to get away with behaving like this.

"The Keepers are too strong," said Omar heavily. "You can't cross them. It's asking for trouble."

"I'm sorry about your van, Omar," said Kit, finally catching up with them, clutching Eppie firmly by the hand. "But we'll have to go home right now. My parents will be beside themselves if they hear about this. And Max needs to tell Bram what's happened."

"Go," said Omar, waving them on their way. "I'll be fine."

Max, Kit and Eppie made their way back across the

beach towards the road, keeping their eyes peeled for any sign of the Keepers. But the place was still and oddly silent, except for the gentle lapping of the waves. Max was silent, trying to think of a way to stop Leandra. Maybe Bram would have some ideas. He seemed to know more about the Keepers than anyone.

He said goodbye to Kit and Eppie once they reached the dusty road that curved above the beach. They hurried back through the village, while he made his way up the steep little lane that led to Bram's farmyard.

Evening had almost fallen by the time he returned. The long shadows meant that for a moment he didn't see the owl that was perched on the stone gatepost, watching him.

It had dark feathers and very piercing orange eyes. As Max approached, it flapped its long wings, blurred for a moment, and then a split-second later it vanished. In its place was Leandra, who was sitting on top of the gatepost and grinning at him in a rather unsettling way.

"Hello," she said, and jumped down, landing on the dusty track with a thud in her leather boots. "It's Max, isn't it?"

She held out her hand, as if she expected him to shake it, but Max kept his own hands firmly by his sides.

"Why are you following me?" he asked, trying to keep his voice steady. The truth was, after what had happened at the beach, he understood why everyone in Yowling was so scared of Leandra. It was terrifying, encountering somebody so unpredictable. She could turn from pleasantries to violence in a heartbeat.

"I'm not interested in you," she said, rolling her eyes and tossing her long dark hair over her shoulder. "It's Bram I want."

"I saw what you did at the beach earlier," said Max coldly. "Why do you have to ruin everything?"

"Because I'm the Keeper of Yowling Castle," said Leandra. "So no one in the village should do anything without asking my permission. Otherwise something very bad will happen to them."

Leandra looked extremely pleased with herself. Max gave up trying to reason with her. It was useless. He remembered what Bram had told him about the castle's magic going bad, and how this had affected the Keepers too. Leandra had clearly become so deluded that she thought she ruled over the whole of Yowling instead of just being the castle's magical caretaker. He turned his back on her and headed towards the farmhouse, but Leandra followed in his footsteps, just a few steps behind him. He stopped. So did she. He started walking again and she began to follow him once more.

"What do you want?" he cried, wheeling around to face her.

"Nothing," she replied, still smiling weirdly.

Max was beginning to feel deeply uneasy. She was playing some sort of game with him, but he didn't know what it was. He hurried towards the kitchen door, wanting to get inside and away from Leandra as quickly as possible. He rattled at the handle, and was surprised to find that it was locked. He peered in through the window, still uncomfortably aware of her presence close behind him, and a moment later Bram threw the door open.

"Thank heavens you're back," he began, ushering Max inside before he could say anything. Then Bram broke off as Leandra darted in behind them and slammed the door shut.

"Got you!" she announced triumphantly, her back pressed to the door.

Bram swore.

"I don't want anything more to do with you!" he bellowed. "Get out of my house!"

But Leandra didn't budge.

"Listen to me," she said firmly. "Or else I'll burn the whole place down."

Leandra drummed her long silver fingernails against the door and looked around the kitchen, her gaze resting firstly on the big wooden dresser and then on the dogs, who were sitting in their feather-filled beds, growling at her. Max had a horrible feeling that she was deciding which of the two to set on fire first. The same thought seemed to have occurred to Bram, as he sank down into the nearest chair and gestured at Leandra to do the same. Max moved protectively towards his grandfather, standing behind his chair, ready to jump to his defence.

"Go on," said Bram, a frown etched upon his face. "Tell me."

"You need to rebalance Yowling Castle," said Leandra, sitting down opposite them and resting her elbows on the table.

"It's impossible," said Bram. "I can't."

"But you can," she said, leaning forwards. "You did it before, remember? Years ago. You agreed to help and you fixed it."

"I almost died in the process," said Bram. "And it ruined my family."

He looked so unhappy that Max sensed that there was more to the story.

"What do you mean, it ruined our family?" he asked, looking at Bram instead of Leandra.

But his grandfather just shook his head and didn't reply.

Max knew that he shouldn't interfere, that it would be better to wait until Leandra had gone before pressing Bram further. But he couldn't stop himself. He remembered that conversation that had taken place between his mother and Bram. She had mentioned the Keeper. Looking back, it was one of the things she'd been most worried about when she had let him go off with Bram.

"Did something happen with my mother?"

Bram looked as if Max had stabbed him.

"He's sharper than he looks," remarked Leandra.

"Shut up!" roared Bram. "You nearly killed my daughter!"

"What?" cried Max. He was so angry he felt like hitting Leandra. "You attacked my mother?"

"I'm sure she'll get over it," replied Leandra airily.

"That was twenty-five years ago," said Bram. "She still hasn't."

"I'd forgotten how long it's been. Time flies, doesn't it?"

She gave another grin, clearly hoping that she could coax Bram into cooperating. When he didn't respond, she dropped her light-hearted manner and scowled at him instead.

"You've got to help," she said. "The castle's worse than I've ever known it. It's never been left this long – I've been asking you to help me for over a year and you keep putting it off. Well you can't any longer. The mist is getting thicker. The whole building shakes, all the time. The floorboards have started to disappear and some of the walls are either so cold or so hot that they'd burn you if you touched them. The magic's going wrong. You need to do something. Right now."

"Not my problem," said Bram.

"It IS your problem!" yelled Leandra, losing her temper. "You're the only one that can fix it!"

"I don't care what happens to that blasted castle," said Bram firmly. "Or you, for that matter."

Leandra stood up very quickly, so that her chair toppled over and crashed to the ground. She was staring at Bram with so much fury that Max wouldn't have been surprised if his grandfather had spontaneously combusted. The three dogs started barking at her, so loudly that the sound was deafening.

"Shut up!" screamed Leandra. She pointed at the dog beds, which burst into flames at once. The dogs yelped and leaped out of them, shooting across the room in terror. Leandra strode over to the door, pushing past Max.

"You'll fix the castle," she said, turning around to give Bram a final blazing look. "Just you wait."

After she had left, and they had thrown potfuls of water over the three burning beds, they were left with a smell of scorched feathers, a wet floor and a distinctly unpleasant atmosphere. At least Treacle, Sardine and Banana were unharmed, except for a couple of patches of slightly singed fur. The dogs were all shocked and subdued – as was Max – but Bram looked the most upset of everyone.

"She's not coming back in here," he growled, and Max heard him going down the steps to the little brick cellar. He reappeared a moment later, carrying an odd contraption that looked like a cross between a rifle and a trumpet.

"What's that?" asked Max, frowning at it.

"Blunderbuss," replied Bram. "If I see another owl, I'm going to shoot it."

"Aren't they too magical for that?" asked Max.

"Probably. But I don't have any better ideas."

"Bram, what did Leandra do to my mother?"

Bram sighed heavily.

"When I went to fix the castle last time, your mother didn't want me to go. She must've been about fourteen at the time. She tried to stop me, but Leandra set the rest of the Keepers on her. They almost ripped her to pieces – it was a miracle she managed to escape without being seriously hurt. And I went over to work on the castle anyway."

"What?" said Max, hardly able to believe it. "You went over there? After Leandra did that?"

"You've got to understand, Max, my family had always helped the castle. It was my grandmother before me, and her great-uncle before that. No one had ever refused before. I felt like I had to. I thought it would be better for everyone in Yowling if I fixed the castle, but I was wrong. I should have left it."

"What did Mum say? After you fixed it?"

"Never forgave me," said Bram miserably.

Max was stunned. He had never guessed that

something like that could have happened to his mother. She seemed so ordinary. There wasn't a single thing about her that suggested her background, that she had grown up in the very same pink bedroom that he was currently sleeping in, with its view of the enchanted castle.

"She left home as soon as she could," continued Bram sadly. "Think she just wanted to get away from it all, really. She was very cut up about not being a spellstopper, you know. Everyone in Yowling has something magical about them, so she felt a bit out of place. Probably best, really, that she built her own life away from all of this. I know she was hoping you wouldn't inherit the gift, but I'm glad you did. It was nice to see her again. And it's good to have you here."

Bram broke off and coughed into his crumpled cotton handkerchief.

"Could you go out and fill some sacks with straw?" he asked. "Dogs need to sleep on something tonight. I'll hunt out a few things for dinner – it'll have to be bread and cheese. Don't think I can face cooking just now."

"Of course," said Max at once, his mind still reeling from what he had just found out.

"Don't worry yourself about anything," advised Bram.

"Like I told your mother, I'm done with the Keepers. All I want is a nice, quiet life."

Max wanted to believe that was possible. But as he trudged across the puddles on the kitchen floor, dragging the charred remains of what had once been three feather-filled dog beds, he had a feeling that things were turning out to be the exact opposite. He was caught up in something much bigger than he had imagined. Whatever Bram said, he knew that Leandra wouldn't let the castle go down without a fight. It made Max want to learn how to spellstop more than ever. Bram was in trouble, that much was clear. And it seemed as if Max was the only person who might be able to help him.

10

Over the next few days, Max noticed a change in his grandfather. He was twitchy and nervous, and refused to answer the door, which caused a lot of confusion for customers. Max kept having nightmares about being attacked – sometimes by the Keepers, but more often by a series of magical objects that he was never able to fix.

These nightmares were at least partly rooted in reality, as Max was spending hours wrestling with the stuffed weasel. It had bitten him repeatedly, and had resisted all attempts to muzzle or restrain it. Max's hands, arms and face were covered in scratches from its needle-sharp claws. Yet, no matter how hard he tried, he couldn't figure out how to spellstop. It seemed impossible.

"You've just got to be patient," said Bram, as Max eyed up the weasel warily. "And—"

"Keep my mind clear," finished Max. "I know."

The weasel, who knew what was coming by now, made a hollow hissing sound then licked its lips.

Max moved towards it warily, trying not to think of anything in particular.

The weasel made a swipe at him, and Max seized both its forepaws in his hands. He felt the magic surge through him, running through his body, then a sudden stabbing sensation broke the connection.

"Ow!" he cried.

The weasel had locked its jaws onto his wrist. Max jerked his arm away, trying desperately to shake it off. It flew across the room, stand and all, hissing furiously as it went, and landed in a pile of blankets at the other end of the workshop, narrowly missing Bram's head and sending the three dogs scurrying out of the way.

Kit was almost crying with laughter and even Bram smiled.

"Oh Max," she gasped, holding on to a bench for support. "That was the best one yet."

"Yeah, hilarious," he replied drily, as he examined his bleeding wrist.

"You'll get there," said Bram, returning the weasel to its usual spot, then passing Max a roll of bandage.

"Although we're out of plasters. Think there's some more in the house."

He ambled out of the workshop, whistling, seeming more like his old self than he'd been since Leandra's visit. A moment later, he returned, slamming the door shut behind him.

"That was quick," said Max, then realized that Bram was empty handed and had a grim, anxious expression on his face.

"What's the matter?" he asked.

Kit looked up from a little wooden doll that she was carefully repainting.

"Owls," said Bram hoarsely. "There's owls outside."

Max made a move towards the door, but Bram stopped him.

"Don't go out there," he said urgently.

Max peered out of the window instead. There was a little white owl sitting on one of the gateposts and a tawny barn owl on the other.

"Do you mean those two?" he asked, pointing them out to Bram and Kit. "Neither of them is Leandra – she was bigger, with black and brown feathers."

"There's more," said Kit. "Look."

A large grey owl was perched on top of Kit's bike,

its talons gripping the handlebars. Half a dozen owls of different shapes and sizes were lined up along the gutter of the house. Three black owls were watching them from the mulberry tree. And there was the owl that Max knew was Leandra, wheeling about in the sky overhead, casting an ominous shadow across the farmyard. All the chickens had vanished. Max guessed that they were hiding somewhere in the barn. At least, he hoped they were.

Bram hurried across the workshop and Max saw that he was holding the ancient blunderbuss, which looked more like a museum piece than a weapon. He inched open the door, took aim, then fired straight at the three owls that were sitting in the mulberry tree. The rusty bang seemed impossibly loud in the confined space of the workshop. Bram staggered backwards, clutching the smoking blunderbuss, but the owls stayed on their perches as if nothing had happened. Bram swore and took aim again, but they just carried on watching him.

"Did you hit them?" asked Max hesitantly.

"Of course I did!" cried Bram, his face creased into a frown.

"Well, they're Keepers," said Kit, as if she was pointing out something incredibly obvious. "They're not like normal birds."

"I'd worked that one out," muttered Bram, as he locked the door again. "Let's just wait in here for a bit, see if they fly off."

Three hours later, the owls were still keeping guard, staring intently at the door to the workshop. The dogs were whining and scratching at the door, wanting to be let out. Max knew how they felt.

"We can't stay in here for ever," he pointed out. "What if we need to use the toilet?"

"There's plenty of empty bottles," replied Bram.

"Urgh," said Kit, making a face. "But I've got to go home soon, anyway."

"Too dangerous," said Bram curtly.

He stared miserably out of the window, and all the owls stared back at him.

"Let me go outside," said Max. "I can see if I can get back into the house. I can get some supplies – we've got nothing to eat or drink in here."

"No!" said Bram. "Those birds could claw you to death in a heartbeat."

Max remembered what Bram had told him about Leandra getting the owls to attack his mother, and knew that his grandfather wasn't exaggerating.

There was a flurry of wings from outside. One of the owls had glided down from the roof and landed just in front of the workshop. It rapped its beak on the door, as if it was asking them to open it, then flew back up to its perch on the old iron guttering.

"What will we do?" whispered Kit, as if she was worried that the owl could hear her.

"Nothing," replied Bram. "We wait."

They waited for what felt like for ever. They waited for so long that they saw the sun move across the sky, turn pink, then finally dip below the horizon. They saw the light fade from the golden shades of dusk to the blue hues of twilight. The owls stayed where they were, still watching them, the huge eagle owl still hovering in the air above.

Bram seemed to have gone into a trance. He simply sat there, in the armchair that Kit had repaired, staring out of the window at the owls. Kit was tidying the workshop. The dogs had gone to sleep. Max, however, was about to crack.

"It's almost dark," he said, his frustration rising. "We've been in here for hours. The owls aren't going to leave now, are they? They love the dark."

He couldn't bear the waiting around any longer – anything would be better than that. He went over to the door and turned the key, unlocking it.

"I'm going outside," he said.

"No!" cried Bram, and he hauled himself up out of the armchair.

But Max was too quick for him. He darted out into the farmyard. All the owls looked at him, but they didn't move.

"Max, come back!" yelled Bram, who was at the door. Kit stood just behind him, staring at Max in shock. Treacle rushed out after Max and grabbed his sleeve with her teeth, trying to tug him back towards the workshop.

"I'm going over to the house," called Max. He was definitely not going to turn around now. He dislodged Treacle and carried on walking.

"Max!" Bram hobbled out after him, closely pursued by Kit and the other two dogs.

As soon as Bram was out in the open, the owls swooped. They all dived on him, crowding around him in a huge fluttering mass, so that he was completely hidden beneath the beating feathered wings.

"Get off him," yelled Max, running at them, waving his arms, trying to scare them. But they ignored him, as if he wasn't worth bothering about. The dogs were yelping and jumping into the air, trying to catch the owls, and Kit was also doing her best to beat them off. None of it worked.

The owls rose up into the air. They had each seized hold of Bram with their talons, all thirteen of them rising as one. Max was yelling as his grandfather's feet rose up off the ground. He tried to grab hold of Bram's legs, to stop him from being carried off, but the little snowy owl pecked him hard, and fluttered its wings in his face, until he lost his grip and staggered backwards. Kit, too, had been knocked to the ground, and by the time she had got to her feet again, Bram was too high up for either of them to reach him.

The owls kept rising as one, up into the air, and then flew off in a gigantic misshapen ball of feathers, with Bram still kicking feebly in their midst. Night was falling, but by the light of the thin sickle moon, Max saw that the birds were heading for the cove, towards the jagged towers of Yowling Castle. His heart twisted in fear at what might happen to Bram. It was all his fault. He had to rescue his grandad.

11

Max and Kit raced after the owls, the dogs at their heels. They left the farmyard and ran down the lane, towards the cove. They lost sight of the birds for a while, as the road dipped downwards, and the hawthorn trees that lined the hedgerows blotted out the night sky. When they finally reached the shore, both gasping for breath, the owls were wheeling about the castle as they usually did, as if nothing had happened. Their black outlines flitted about like bats under the pale light of the moon, while below them the green mist swirled ceaselessly, looking eerier than ever.

"They must have left him somewhere in the castle," said Max, straining his eyes to see better, but the castle was too far away and it was too dark to see anything properly, in any case. They stopped when they reached the damp sand, just above where the tide lapped in and out. The dogs edged forwards, their noses down, as if they couldn't quite decide if they should go into the sea or not.

"What do we do now?" asked Kit, turning to Max.

"There has to be some way to get across," he said, looking around desperately, hoping to catch sight of something or someone that could help them. But all was silent and still.

"Why aren't there any boats?" he asked, as it struck him that the pier and harbour were completely empty.

Kit just raised her eyebrows at him and Max felt stupid for even asking, as he looked across at the owls circling the pointed turrets. The castle suddenly seemed like a vast distance away. What hope did he and Kit have of rescuing Bram from a place like that? He should never have left the workshop. It was all his fault that Bram had been taken. He started to imagine all the bad things that could be happening to his grandfather at that moment and he felt sick. He realized for the first time how close he'd grown to Bram, even though he'd only been staying with him for a short while. His grandfather had made his life so much bigger and more exciting than it had ever been before. The idea of him suffering was unbearable.

"Leandra needs Bram to help her with the castle,

remember?" said Kit, who seemed to have guessed his thoughts. "So he'll be safe."

"Bram said that fixing the castle would kill him," said Max flatly.

"I've an idea," said Kit suddenly. "Let's go and see the Captain."

"Who?"

"He lives close by," said Kit. "If anyone knows where to get hold of a boat, he will. He used to be a ship's captain – he's been in Yowling for longer than anyone can remember. Everyone just calls him the Captain – I've no idea what his real name is."

They called the dogs, who had scattered around the beach, sniffing intently as if they were trying to track down Bram. Then Kit led the way underneath the rickety wooden pier, across the sands and up to the seafront, then down along the row of squashed-together houses until she stopped in front of one that looked as if it had been made out of part of an old ship. Its front was studded with criss-crossed timber beams, and an old figurehead sat above the door, carved into the shape of a woman, who looked blankly out towards the sea. The house's upper windows were round and appeared to have been made from old portholes. The curved bay windows on the ground floor were covered with tattered curtains, but a light shone though one of them, signalling that somebody was inside.

Kit knocked on the door and Max stood next to her, holding Banana and Sardine by their collars. Unlike Treacle, who was older and more sensible, the two younger dogs tended to be over-enthusiastic in greeting people.

Kit knocked for a second time, then when nobody answered, she poked open the rusty letter box and peered through it.

"Hello?" she called. "Are you in?"

A moment later, the door creaked open a fraction.

"Don't shout!" hissed a voice. "She'll hear you!"

"She's in the castle," said Kit.

"What makes you so certain of that?" replied the Captain, still hiding behind the door.

"Because she's just taken Bram!" said Kit. "Me and Max – his grandson – just saw it happen. The rest of the Keepers carried him off."

The door shot open and an arm pulled Kit inside. It reached out for Max, but stopped suddenly.

"You've brought dogs?"

A man with a pale, scarred face peered around the

edge of the door. He was wearing a large, voluminous shirt with yellowed lace sleeves, trousers that ended just below the knee, dusty white stockings and a pair of heavily embroidered slippers. He was quite old but his hair was long and curled. He might have been wearing a wig. The overall effect was impressive and Max couldn't stop staring.

"They're not coming in."

"But I can't leave them outside," protested Max.

"I'll get you some string," said the man. He padded off down the corridor and presently returned with a large ball of twine and an old-fashioned penknife. "You can tie them to the railings."

Max did so. Treacle seemed resigned to staying there, but Banana and Sardine kept whining and straining against the string, staring up at him as if he was abandoning them.

"I'll be back soon," he promised, then followed the man inside.

It was an interesting house. The hallway was plastered from floor to ceiling with paintings – nearly all of them of shipwrecks. The floorboards creaked loudly and they all sloped in different directions, which made you walk in an uneven, lurching way, almost as if you were on a ship. It smelled of a mixture of stale tobacco and equally stale fish, which wasn't particularly pleasant to start with, but got less noticeable over time. Kit was in the sitting room, where there was a roaring fire in a big open hearth. There were no shipwreck paintings here. Instead the walls were hung with a collection of faded ships' flags, and lots of hand-drawn maps of oceans that Max didn't recognize. There was also a pigeon perched on top of a tallboy, nestled into a velvet cushion. It stood up when Max came in and peered down at him, blinking sleepily, then settled back down again and closed its eyes.

"Sit down, sit down," said the Captain, gesturing to the lumpy armchairs that were grouped in front of the fire, and Max lowered himself into a chair whose seat sunk violently downwards. It was a bit like sitting in a bucket. The Captain threw a large log onto the fire, which sent showers of sparks shooting up the chimney, then stood directly in front of the hearth, warming his back. Max thought that he looked oddly faint, but perhaps it was just a trick of the firelight.

"Well, then," said the Captain. "Tell me what happened."

Max glanced at Kit, not sure if they should, but she nodded.

"We can trust the Captain," she said. "He doesn't like the Keepers either."

The Captain spluttered.

"Of course I don't!" he roared. "Who in Yowling does?"

He settled himself back against the mantlepiece more comfortably, then pointed to the large carved narwhal horn that hung in pride of place on the opposite wall.

"Bram spellstopped that for me fifteen years ago," he said. "It had got so bad it nearly drove me mad. Kept whistling, all the time. It wouldn't desist, no matter what I did. Bram put it right in a jiffy – he wouldn't even take any payment for it. I'm indebted to him – you can trust me."

Max was reassured. He and Kit recounted exactly what had happened. When they had finished, the Captain looked serious.

"So he's imprisoned in the castle now then?" he asked. "Just him and the owls?"

They nodded.

"Well," he said. "You did right coming straight to me. I know Yowling Cove better than anyone. I've sailed every inch of it."

"Is there a way into the castle?" asked Kit. "Have you been inside?"

"I've never been inside, but I do know of a way in. There's a door – it's hidden right at the back of the castle, facing the rocks."

Max and Kit exchanged hopeful looks.

"What about a boat?" asked Max. "Can you help us get out there?"

"A boat?" roared the Captain, startling the pigeon, who fluttered off the tallboy and flew up to the safety of the curtain pole. "I used to command an entire fleet. Of course I can help you with a boat."

Max grinned.

"But what will we do when we get there?" asked Kit, who was clearly hoping for a more detailed plan.

"One thing at a time, young Kit," replied the Captain. "I'll ferry you over there, that's all I can promise. Give me a couple of hours and I'll send word once we're ready to mount an attack."

The Captain looked quite delighted at the prospect of an adventure. He gave a cooing whistle and the pigeon flew down from the curtain rail and landed on his outstretched arm, just below his lacy shirt cuffs.

"This is Cassandra," said the Captain proudly. "Beautiful, isn't she?"

"Lovely," agreed Max, wanting to keep him happy,

despite having no idea of whether Cassandra was a good-looking pigeon or not.

The Captain beamed with pleasure, and stroked the pigeon with his forefinger, while she pecked at his curled hair.

"I found her as a hatchling, squawking all by herself in the middle of the street," he said. "I saved her from being eaten by a seagull. I thought she'd fly off once she was grown, but she prefers to stay with me. It's no wonder, really. Pigeons are very intelligent birds."

Cassandra stared at them intently as the Captain ushered Max and Kit back through the hall again.

"I need to arrange a few things," he said. "I'll have everything shipshape before you know it."

"We don't have much time," said Max, who already felt that things were moving too slowly. "Anything could be happening to Bram."

"I'll be as quick as I can," said the Captain firmly. "If all goes well, we'll be off before daybreak."

"I'll go home and get some supplies," Kit said to Max. "We need to be as prepared as we can. Also, I should have been home hours ago. You can come with me if you like."

"I'll drop the dogs back at Bram's," said Max. "And everything's just been left open – the workshop, the house. If we have to wait, it's better if I go back, sort things out."

"Right you are," said the Captain. "I'll send word when we're ready to set sail."

They thanked him and went outside, back into the night. Max untied the dogs, while Kit looked at him uncertainly.

"Are you sure you'll be all right on your own?" she asked.

"Of course," said Max firmly, even though the idea of being at the farmhouse by himself felt very peculiar.

Kit still looked a bit uncertain, but after Max had repeated that he really would be fine, she said goodnight and headed up the narrow steps, through the winding streets towards her house. Max started to pull the dogs in the other direction, and headed back to the empty farmhouse by the light of the moon, his eyes fixed on the jagged silhouette of the castle that loomed above the glimmering dark sea.

"We're coming to rescue you," he said out loud, wishing there was some way that Bram could hear him. "You'll be home by morning."

He tried to ignore the gnawing lump of worry that was clawing at his insides. He had to be brave. Bram needed him.

12

The rest of the night was awful. Max paced about the empty farmhouse, sick with worry, half-expecting Bram to reappear at any moment. But he didn't, of course. The house felt different without his grandfather there – it had an unsettled, hushed atmosphere, as if the building itself was upset. Max went up to his bedroom and sat on the window seat, staring out into the darkness at the spot where he knew the castle was, wishing for dawn to come.

He woke up very suddenly to the sound of something tapping on his bedroom window. A small grey pigeon was perched on the windowsill, rapping its beak on the glass. It still seemed to be the middle of the night, as the sun wasn't up. The pigeon continued to knock at the window until Max reached over and opened it. It stuck out its leg and Max saw that there was a little roll of paper attached to it.

Come to the cove at once, the message said, in swirly, old-fashioned writing.

Max guessed that it was from the Captain and the pigeon was Cassandra. He left the window open, in case she wanted to come inside, but as soon as Max had read the note she flew off, back towards the village.

Max rushed downstairs at once, not wanting to waste a moment. The dogs woke up when he hurried through the kitchen, and he felt a slight pang at leaving them in the house. He knew that taking them would be a bad idea – quite apart from the Captain's aversion to dogs, he suspected that it would be safer for them to stay put, given what Leandra had done last time she saw them. They stared at him reproachfully through the kitchen window as he left the yard, their noses pressed to the glass.

Even though the sun hadn't yet risen, the first glow of daylight was starting to appear. Kit was already at the cove, waiting for him. She was wearing a waterproof coat and had a large backpack slung across her shoulders, as if she was about to set off on a hike.

"What's in there?" asked Max, pointing at it.

"Supplies," she said, practical as ever. "First aid kit, compass, a penknife, a blanket, string, a torch, dog food, water and some biscuits."

"I didn't bring anything," admitted Max, who was feeling underprepared by comparison. "But what's the dog food for, anyway? I left the dogs at Bram's."

"It's only for emergencies," said Kit mysteriously. "Hopefully we won't need it. Come on – the Captain's over by the pier."

They hurried across the sand, and Max could see the castle now, silhouetted against the dark sky. For once, there was no sign of the birds flitting about the turrets.

"How long do you think we've got before the owls come back?"

"Until the sun comes up fully," said Kit. "They're hunting in the woods over there. Even old Keepers need to eat. Hopefully we'll have rescued Bram and be back here by the time they find out what's happened."

"Do you think Leandra goes with them?" asked Max.

"I think she probably does," said Kit thoughtfully. "She definitely doesn't buy food from the village, and she must eat something. Imagine, Leandra eating mice."

She shuddered.

They were nearly at the pier now and up ahead they saw the Captain standing next to a large lumpy shape covered with some sacking. He looked even paler, somehow, now that he was outside – his skin was oddly pearlescent. But he waved cheerfully as soon as he saw them.

"Excellent news," he cried. "Getting a boat proved more challenging than I'd anticipated, but I prevailed in the end."

He pulled the sacking off with a flourish. Max's heart sank. It was Tom's rowing boat. The hole in the bottom had been roughly patched up with a length of wood and a bit of tar. Kit frowned at the repair, clearly unimpressed.

"Good as new," announced the Captain.

Something large and fish-like erupted from the sand right beside Max.

"Tom!" croaked Max, reeling from the shock.

"Yurp," said Tom, by way of greeting.

"Tom's coming with us," said the Captain. "Between us, we know every inch of that bay. We'll see you over safely."

This was not exactly how Max had imagined their rescue mission, setting off with them all crammed into Tom's broken rowing boat. But the Captain looked so enthusiastic that it seemed pointless to argue, especially since they had no better alternative.

"Present for you," Tom was saying to Kit. "For fixing those pots. Here."

He thrust an unhappy wriggling lobster into Kit's hands.

"Er…thanks," said Kit, holding the lobster at arm's length and looking uncomfortable. It was waving its claws in the air and clicking them furiously. She set it down in the boat and it immediately hid itself beneath a sack. "I'll just keep it there for now."

"Hurry!" cried the Captain. "The sooner we go, the better. There's no point waiting for those owls to come back. The tide's too low to use the pier – we'll have to launch our vessel the hard way."

This meant that all four of them had to shove the boat down the beach until they got to the water.

"You two young ones jump in now," instructed the Captain. "We'll push it out."

Max and Kit clambered into the boat and settled themselves on a wooden bench towards the back, taking care not to disturb the lobster. Max watched Tom, steadily pushing the boat out to sea, while the Captain danced about him, calling out instructions, but not actually doing anything. They waded forwards, until the boat stopped rasping against the sand and floated on the waves. The boat lurched from side to side as Tom hefted himself in, clambering over the side, but the Captain vaulted in elegantly, as if he weighed nothing at all. There was something peculiar about him, but Max couldn't quite put his finger on it.

"Right," said the Captain, handing Tom an oar and taking the other one himself. "Off we go."

The Captain hauled at his oar, but his hands slipped right through the wood. He tried again, but the same thing happened. Meanwhile, Tom had started to row with gusto, and the boat began to turn in circles.

"Stop!" cried Max, as they lurched about. "What's the matter?"

"Tom's rowing out of time," said the Captain. "It's a common mistake with novice oarsmen."

He took hold of his own oar again and spoke kindly to Tom.

"Just try and keep pace with me," he said. "And heave!"

Tom's oar cut through the water, while the Captain's hands slipped through his own oar yet again. Max caught Kit's eye and she shrugged at him, clearly equally at a loss.

"Tom!" said the Captain, in a reproving, fatherly way. "Let's have another attempt – I'm sure you'll master it eventually."

Tom looked annoyed. His fish-like eyes boggled at the

Captain and his knuckles tightened around his own oar. Max, meanwhile, was beginning to get suspicious. It was all starting to make sense – the Captain's oddly translucent appearance, the way his hands kept slipping through solid objects, the fact that his strange house looked as if time had stood still for several centuries.

"You're a ghost, aren't you?" he said, addressing the Captain directly.

"So what if I am?" replied the Captain. "I've sailed round the world six times – how many of you can say you've done the same?"

"But you can't row!" cried Max in exasperation, conscious of how much time they were wasting.

"Of course I can!" retorted the Captain, looking deeply affronted. "I was a champion oarsman in my day."

Tom seized the opportunity to grab the Captain's oar as well as his own and began to row with swift, steady strokes. The Captain shuffled backwards out of the way, and frowned for a moment, watching him.

"Well, you seem to have found your stride now," he admitted grudgingly. "Some men work best on their own." He folded his arms, watching Tom critically.

"Didn't you know the Captain was a ghost?" Max whispered to Kit.

"No!" she hissed back. "I've never seen him outside before. And you don't just go round asking people in Yowling what they are – it's considered really rude. If they don't tell you, you just have to accept not knowing."

They lapsed into silence as they headed out into the bay. The little boat bobbed across the waves and the castle got bigger and bigger the further out they went, as did the line of tall spiky rocks that stood behind it, cutting off the cove from the open sea beyond. It was getting colder now they were out on the water, and Max shivered in his thin jumper, especially as he kept getting splashed from the strokes of the oars.

It was cloudy and overcast, so the sea was the same slate grey as the sky and the castle looked blacker and more sinister than ever, wreathed by the ghoulish green mist that swirled ceaselessly about it.

Max leaned forwards, peering around Tom to get a better view. The castle was set on a mound of jagged rock and was even more enormous than he had originally thought. There were at least a dozen turrets, all with narrow slit windows. The side that faced the bay had no visible door and the lowest windows were at least six metres above the rock. Max thought that it looked like a prison. Bram's chances of escaping seemed increasingly slim.

"Don't get too close," the Captain said to Tom. "Keep a wide berth as we row round – we don't know what that dratted mist might do."

"How will we get through it?" asked Max.

"You're the spellstoppers," replied the Captain. "I was expecting you two to have thought of that."

Max and Kit exchanged dismayed looks. Max had still had no success whatsoever at spellstopping anything. If magical intervention was required, they were definitely in trouble.

"Let's just wait and see," said Kit at last. "It mightn't be as bad once we get around to the other side."

They all watched apprehensively as they made their way around the edge of the castle. The waves lapped against the sides of the boat and the oars creaked as they swung to and fro.

"Here we go," said the Captain as they rounded the corner. They bobbed down a narrow choppy strip with the castle on one side of them and the line of rocks on the other. The narrow inlet felt very oppressive and Max's skin prickled with fear. He could tell by the faces of the other three that they were feeling the same. Even the Captain had lost some of his hearty manner.

"That's the spot," he said, in an unusually subdued

voice, pointing at the rear of the castle. There, above them, in the curving wall of one of the turrets, was a narrow black arch the size of a door, cut into the stone.

"Could you bring the boat a bit closer?" Max asked. "We'll have to climb up there."

Tom guided the boat until it bumped along the edge of the rough rocky mound at the base of the castle, ducking down to avoid the mist that swirled above their heads.

"I'm not sure about going through it," said Kit, frowning up at the mist.

"Can I borrow an oar?" asked Max, and Tom handed one over.

Max held it up in the air and waved it through the green mist. Nothing happened. He stood up, slowly, to avoid rocking the boat, and then raised his arm up too. The mist felt oddly warm compared to the chilly morning air, but apart from that, it seemed to have no effect at all.

"I think it's fine," he said. He ignored the thudding of his heart as he examined the steep craggy rock face for handholds. He wedged one foot into a shallow crevice and grabbed hold of a slimy spur. Then he stepped up, out of the boat.

"Tom and I will stay on board," announced the Captain. Now that they had reached the castle, the Captain's face was gleaming bright white with fear. "We'll make sure the vessel's shipshape for a speedy return."

"Yurp," agreed Tom.

"Will you wait here for us?" asked Kit, who had got to her feet too.

"Of course!" cried the Captain. "Never abandon a shipmate – that's my motto."

Max began to climb steadily upwards, straining his eyes to see, his hands and feet slipping on the wet rocks. Kit followed, just below him. Within seconds he was enveloped in the green swirling mist.

As Max breathed in mouthfuls of the warm mist, he felt his mind beginning to go foggy. He kept climbing, stumbling now as he went.

"Max," said Kit, who had drawn level with him. "I'm beginning to feel dizzy."

"Me too," he said, finding it hard to even form the words.

His brain seemed to get more sluggish by the second and he almost fell as he missed a foothold. Kit made it up to the top of the rocks and collapsed at once into a ball, covering her face with her hands. With a huge effort,

Max hauled himself to the top and crawled forwards to where Kit was.

"My head," she moaned.

"Keep going," said Max thickly, forcing himself onto his feet. "It's clear up in front."

The two of them staggered forwards across the uneven ground and out of the mist. Their heads cleared instantly.

"What was that?" said Kit, looking back at the mist. It was so dense that it clouded out the view of the sea below, and its greenish tinge made everything seem sickly and odd.

But Max was staring towards the castle, unable to believe his eyes.

The door had vanished. There was just smooth dark stone in the place where the arch had been.

"I thought it was straight in front of us," he said, scanning the side of the high castle wall. "It's disappeared!"

He and Kit started to edge their way along the perimeter of the castle, around the curved towers, looking frantically for a door. But there was none to be found. Instead, they were just hit by more waves of the green mist. They slipped and tripped on the wet uneven rocks, getting more and more dizzy and confused. It began to feel as if they weren't even there at all, as if it was just a bad dream. Then Kit gave a cry as her foot slipped on a loose rock. Her heavy backpack made her unable to regain her balance, and before Max could do anything to help her, she fell straight over the edge, through the green clouds, towards the sea.

13

"Kit!" yelled Max, as he ran towards the edge of the rocks, his feet slipping on the slimy algae, his head pounding from the mist that still swirled around him, clouding his vision and making everything look green and strange.

He peered over the edge, straining his eyes to see. There, on the rocks below, just above the level of the waves, was Kit. She was moving, but he couldn't make out if she was hurt or not. He began to scramble down to join her, but as his head was still spinning, he lost his grip and half-slid, half-fell down the steep rocks and landed heavily beside her.

"Are you okay?" asked Kit, staggering over to him. She had grazed the side of her face and one of her hands, but otherwise seemed unhurt.

"Yes!" replied Max, his head clearing at once now that they were below the level of the mist. He scrambled to his feet and stared at her. "It was you I was worried about! You fell straight over the edge."

"It wasn't that bad," she replied. "I grabbed hold of a rock going down – that broke my fall. And my backpack gave me a soft landing. I knew it was a good idea to bring a blanket."

"Ahoy there!" came a voice, and they saw the Captain and Tom heading towards them in the little rowing boat. Tom was rowing stoically, while the Captain perched in the bow.

"Hold on!" called the Captain. "We're coming over."

The boat bobbed closer, then bumped against the side of the rocks. Kit and Max clambered aboard and the boat lurched violently.

"Is there another way in?" asked Max, at once. He was very aware that their rescue mission was not going to plan, and kept anxiously scanning the sky in case the owls returned. "Let's row around the other side – we might spot something."

He stood up to get a better look at the castle, craning his head to look up at the steep dark walls. There, high above him, a face was peering out of one of the tower windows. It was so far away that Max couldn't quite make out the features properly. But there was something very familiar about the mass of grizzled grey hair and the thick bushy eyebrows.

"Bram!" he yelled, almost toppling overboard. "BRAM!"

"Max?" cried Bram, his hoarse voice carrying on the breeze. "Kit?"

"We've come to rescue you!" shouted Max. "How do we get in? We can't find a door!"

But Bram was waving his arms frantically, signalling them to turn back.

"The Keepers are coming!" he bellowed and pointed at the horizon. "Get away from here! Go back to the shore, quick!"

Max turned and saw that there was a mass of owls flying out of the woods, silhouetted against the breaking dawn.

"Isn't there some other way in?" he yelled desperately. "We can't leave you in there!"

"THERE'S NO OTHER WAY!" Bram shouted at the top of his voice. "JUST GO! OR THEY WILL KILL YOU!"

Max sat back down, stunned by their bad luck.

Kit, meanwhile, was frowning at Tom and the Captain.

"What's the matter with the boat?" she asked urgently.

"Ah," said the Captain uncomfortably. "The thing is, we seem to have a bit of a problem." He gestured towards Tom, who had spread his anorak over part of the bottom of the boat and was using both feet to press it in place. He was scooping up water with a tin bucket and emptying it over the side.

"The repair wasn't quite as watertight as we'd hoped," admitted the Captain, looking rather guilty.

Max's heart sank even further as he realized that water was seeping in through the bottom of the boat. Kit scrambled forwards to where Tom was sitting, lifted up the corner of the anorak and examined the hole.

"That whole repair is coming loose," she said, in a hollow voice. "The water's getting in everywhere."

"We'll row back quickly," said the Captain, sounding panicked. "It'll be fine – perhaps you two could take over from Tom with plugging the hole and bailing us out."

"WHAT ARE YOU WAITING FOR?" bellowed Bram, from high above them. "THEY'RE COMING FOR YOU!"

Tom started to row frantically. Max grabbed the bucket and started scooping up the water that was now beginning to slosh around his ankles.

"It's not working," said Kit in frustration, pressing the

anorak over the hole in the boat, her teeth gritted as the water kept surging in.

"It's waterproof, isn't it?" bellowed the Captain, losing his composure at last. "Just keep it over the hole! It's better than nothing!"

Kit made a face, but continued to hold back the sea with Tom's anorak while Max continued bailing. The boat was out of the channel now and was heading away from the rocks, back around the side of the castle. The lobster crawled out from beneath the seat at the back of the boat, clicking its claws. Kit quickly seized it and dropped it over the side while Tom wasn't looking.

Then there was a loud cry and a shadow flitted across the boat. Max glanced up then ducked as an owl flew at his head, its claws outstretched. The whole sky suddenly seemed to be full of them, as they gathered above the boat like a dark cloud. Another one swooped down, and this time Max felt its talons graze his shoulders. He yelled and hit it as hard as he could with the bucket. It shot off, screeching, then rejoined the mass of owls that continued to hover above them.

Their situation was getting worse by the second. The sea was now almost halfway up the inside of the boat. Tom was still grimly rowing at full speed, but because of the weight of the water they were going slower and slower.

"It's going to sink," said Kit, abandoning the anorak and trying to scoop out armfuls of water instead. "We're not going to get to the shore in time."

Two more owls dive-bombed them, and once again, Max whacked them away.

"Maybe we should swim," he said, not taking his eyes off the owls for a moment. "We might shake off the Keepers. The boat's going down anyway."

"But there's all sorts of creatures down there," said the Captain in horror. "What about the mugfish?"

"Mugfish?" Max frowned impatiently.

"They look like really big goldfish, but they feed on humans," said Kit. "The minute we're in there, they'll smell us. But the owls will get us before the mugfish do. Being in the sea will just make it easier for them to pick us off."

She spoke in a very matter-of-fact voice, but her lip trembled. For once, even Kit seemed at a loss.

But Max had an idea.

"What if we flip the boat over?" he suggested, as he swiped at another attacking owl. "Once it's upside down it should float – it won't matter if there's a hole in the bottom. We can swim along underneath it – we can even

166

hang on to the seats to stay afloat. That way, it'll be harder for the owls to get at us. And if we're quick, we might be back on dry land before the fish find us."

"Of course!" said Kit, her face clearing. "I can't believe I didn't think of that!"

She sprang into action at once, stowing her backpack into the space where the lobster had been, then tossing the oars overboard, out of the way, so that they bobbed along on top of the waves. Then she came over to join Max, so that the boat started to lean to one side. Tom shifted his weight across too, and the boat gave another violent heave. It was completely unbalanced now, and even more water sloshed in. Two shrieking owls flew at them, and they all ducked quickly.

"What about me?" protested the Captain, who was eyeing the water in horror, and clutching at the edge of the tilting boat. "What am I supposed to do?"

"Swim!" said Kit.

"I'm a sailor," cried the Captain. "Sailors don't learn how to swim – it's unlucky!"

"Just hold onto the side, and it won't matter if you can swim or not!" retorted Max, who was losing his patience with the Captain. "Besides, it's not like you're going to drown! You're a ghost, remember?"

Tom put an end to the debate by rocking the boat violently, just as the entire flock of birds flew at them in one angry mass of feathers, their claws outstretched and sharp. The boat tipped over with a dramatic lurch and Max held his breath as they all sank down under the water. The cold sea hit him like a blow and straight afterwards there was a loud splash as the upturned boat hit the waves. Max rose to the surface, gasping, and ducked underneath it. He was only just in time – the owls screeched and dived at him, and he heard their beaks drum against the rowing boat's wooden boards.

"You made it!" exclaimed Kit, who was already holding on to the plank seat as if it was a float. He joined her, hardly able to see in the dim light that trickled in through the hole in the boat's hull. There was a thud as something landed on the top of the boat. Max heard a clacking, scraping noise – the sound of claws on wood. Then a pair of yellow eyes peered through the hole. Kit sank down into the water so only her face was visible, and Max did the same, feeling the salt water stinging his eyes and seeping up his nose. The owl clawed at the splintered edges of the hole, but was too large to fit through. It started pecking at the hole with its beak, then to Max's horror, more owls joined in. Bits of wood started to shower down on them as the mass of owls slowly began to tear the boat apart.

Then a loud bang came from the direction of the castle. At once, there was a flurry of wings, and all the birds flew off.

Max and Kit bobbed up again, resting their arms on the seat.

"I bet that was Bram," gasped Kit. "He must have seen us go down and caused a diversion."

The relief Max felt at the Keepers' departure evaporated when he imagined how Leandra might punish his grandfather for trying to help them.

"Where are the others?" asked Kit, breaking into his thoughts. "Do you think they made it?"

Just then, the Captain surfaced, with much spluttering, supported by Tom. Max noticed that Tom's hands – which had always been quite frog-like – had grown even bigger and were now fully webbed. He also had gills and looked more like a fish than ever. Tom shoved the Captain, who was burbling unhappily, onto the small ledge next to Kit's backpack. Then he seized the stern of the rowing boat and began to swim strongly, pushing it along, while staying underwater. The boat started to glide forwards, surprisingly fast, and

Max and Kit swam side by side, holding on to the wooden bench.

But just when Max began to think they were out of danger, he felt something tugging at his legs. He twisted away, then Kit gave a yell too.

"They've found us," she cried, and gave a huge kick.

"Told you," muttered the Captain from his corner, as he wedged himself more tightly into the tiny space between the upturned seat and the boat's curved hull, compressing himself in a way that no living person could.

Something seized Max's ankle and held onto it firmly. He was pulled down under the water and saw that a huge orange fish was attached to his foot. It took all of Max's strength to force its jaws open and wrench himself free. His shoe was in tatters. The fish's mouth was rubbery and toothless, but Max could see spiralling rows of sharp teeth running the whole way down its throat. It wasn't alone, either. Half a dozen other fish were milling about the boat, each of them looking very hungry.

Tom goggled at Max in alarm, and kicked even harder with his webbed feet, sending the boat shooting forwards. Max only just managed to grab hold of the seat again, but he could see the fish making grabs at him.

"My backpack!" yelled Kit, splashing over towards the Captain, who pushed it towards her. He tried picking it up, but his hands slipped right through it.

"Sorry," he said in apologetic tones. "I get fainter when I'm nervous."

Kit ripped open the zip, rummaged about and pulled out the tin of dog food. She yanked on the ring pull and peeled back the lid with trembling hands, then shook the entire contents of the tin into the water.

At once, there was a flurry of glimmering orange as the whole shoal of mugfish shot after the meat, swimming down into the watery depths.

"There's only one thing that mugfish prefer to humans, and that's dog food," said Kit, as the others stared at her.

"How on earth did you know that?" said Max faintly.

"Dad," she said simply. "He spends half his life in the sea, remember?"

"Well, thank Jove you're so resourceful, young Kit," cried the Captain, in cheerful tones. "Onwards, Tom!"

Tom propelled the boat along faster than ever, until it finally reached the shallows and bumped against the seabed. They emerged from underneath the boat, blinking at being out in the daylight. Somehow, they managed to haul the rowing boat up onto the shore, then all four of them collapsed onto the sand.

Max felt his initial relief at being back on dry land ebb away, as he remembered that Bram was not only still in the castle, but was probably now in an even worse situation, thanks to their rescue attempt. He didn't know what sort of diversion Bram had created, but it must have put him in greater danger.

Despair washed over Max. He had no idea what to do now. He wished that he'd learned how to spellstop – at least that would have given him some sort of magical ability. Instead, he felt completely powerless. Visions of what might be happening to Bram kept flickering through his mind like some horrible film. Max got to his feet, soaked to the skin and exhausted. He knew he needed another plan, and soon. The problem was, he had absolutely no clue what that plan should be.

14

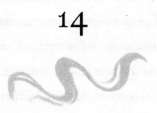

"We need to get off the beach," said Kit, who was surveying the horizon with a frown. "It's too dangerous – the Keepers might come after us again."

Max followed her gaze and saw that the owls were still flitting about the castle turrets, above the mist that looked even thicker and greener than before. He knew that Kit was right. They were asking for trouble being out in the open, in full view of the castle. Bram wouldn't be able to distract the owls for ever.

"Let's go back to my house," suggested Kit, slinging her sodden backpack over her shoulders. She turned to the others. "You can come too, if you like."

"Best be off," said Tom, shaking his head and looking embarrassed.

And he sank down into the sand.

"I'll have to decline too," said the Captain. "Cassandra will be waiting for me."

Out of all of them, the Captain looked the most bedraggled. His wig was askew, one of his lace sleeves was torn and you could see right through him. Max had no idea how ghosts responded to stress, but the Captain certainly seemed to be suffering.

"Will you be all right?" he asked.

"I'll be fit as a fiddle, don't you worry," said the Captain. "I just need a bit of a rest – my sea legs aren't what they used to be."

He raised a hand in a farewell salute and drifted off in the direction of his house.

"So what do we do now?" asked Kit, as she and Max hurried towards the village.

"Try again," said Max, trying to sound more confident than he felt.

"But how?" asked Kit, frowning. "You heard Bram – he said there wasn't any other way in."

Max fell silent. He didn't have an answer, and the more he thought about it, the more impossible it seemed.

They were heading up the main street now. Something looked different, but Max couldn't quite figure out what it was.

Then Kit nudged him, and pointed to what had once been the boarded-up shopfront that concealed Pearl's bakery.

"The cafe," breathed Kit. "She's actually opened it."

The old, dilapidated building that had stood next to Pearl's shop had been completely transformed. The outside of it had been painted a cheery lemon yellow, and the windows had been cleaned until they sparkled. Inside, lines of colourful bunting framed a rainbow display of glass cake stands that were piled high with cakes and pastries. Behind it were tables of people, eating and laughing. Pearl appeared at the window, waved, then rushed over and threw open the door.

"What happened to you both?" she cried. "You're soaked to the skin!"

"We went swimming," said Kit evasively.

"In your clothes?" asked Pearl, looking bemused. "Why don't you come inside and dry off."

"What made you open the cafe?" asked Max, as she ushered them inside.

"Well everyone's been talking about what happened to Bram. It made me think how dreadful it's become, living here. So I decided to open the cafe. Someone needs to stand up to Leandra. And I thought that if I did something, perhaps it might encourage other people to stand up to her too."

As Max looked around the cafe, he realized he had never seen so many of the villagers in one place before. Almost all of the little round tables were occupied. A delicious scent of freshly baked cakes wafted through the air and there was a happy hum of voices and the clink of cutlery on china, which died away rather abruptly as Max and Kit arrived. Everyone seemed to be staring at them.

"I can fix that, if you like," said Pearl, and Max realized that he and Kit were dripping sea water all over the sandy floor.

She whispered something under her breath and waved her hands about in a funny circular motion. Max felt his clothes dry at once. It was the strangest feeling, as if the water had just evaporated.

"Thanks," he said in surprise.

"It'll wear off as soon as you leave, I'm afraid," said Pearl, sounding apologetic. "But at least it means you can stay for something to eat."

"We should really go—" began Max, who felt like the most important thing was to rescue Bram, but Kit interrupted him.

"We'd love to," she said brightly and then turned to Max.

"We might as well," she said in a low voice. "We need to figure out what to do next."

Pearl showed them to a table and hurried off, returning with a tray laden with lemonade, ginger beer and a staggering selection of pastries and cakes. Max recognized the ones shaped like scallop shells and sea urchins, but there were others he hadn't seen before.

"Those are chocolate conches and these ones are seashore surprises," announced Pearl, pointing them out as she placed everything on the table. "I've got to see to the other customers, but call me if you want anything else."

She left, and Max took a bite out of a seashore surprise, a lemon-coloured iced cake that was shaped rather like a small crab. He chewed thoughtfully, so absorbed with trying to come up with a plan that he barely noticed when his seashore surprise wriggled out of his hands and hid behind his lemonade bottle.

"The only thing I can think of is learning how to spellstop," he said. "Bram wanted me to, after all. Maybe it could help in some way."

Kit was clasping a ginger beer and looking equally preoccupied.

"Being able to spellstop didn't keep Bram from being taken though," she said. "And he looked pretty trapped when we saw him in the castle, didn't he?"

Annoying though it was, Max had to admit that Kit had a point. But he still felt as if it was something he had to do. Instead of replying, he tried to recapture his seashore surprise. It let out a high-pitched squeak and jumped off the table, scurried across the floor and hid underneath the counter. Max abandoned any hope of retrieving the runaway cake and turned back to Kit.

"What if we asked the people in here if they know of a way into the castle?" he asked.

"We can't!" Kit looked scandalized. "Everyone in Yowling's terrified of Leandra – you can't just come out with something like that. You've got to be careful about who you speak to."

But Max was already getting to his feet. It had to be worth a try.

"Hello?" he called, as loudly as he could. The whole cafe fell silent once more as everybody turned to stare at him.

"I need your help," he began. "My grandfather's been taken by the Keepers – he's trapped in the castle. Does anyone know how I could reach him? Is there any way in?"

A man covered in silvery scales choked on his coffee. An elderly woman with long greenish hair that looked like seaweed had a forkful of cake suspended in mid-air, as if she was too surprised to put it in her mouth. A stout man with a long black beard and a lumpy fisherman's jersey that reached to his knees opened his mouth then shut it again. However, nobody said a word.

"We've got to stand up to Leandra!" Max cried. "Pearl's been brave – she's opened this cafe and you all came. Bram will die if Leandra makes him fix the castle again. I just need to find a way in, so I can get him out of there."

He looked around the room expectantly. He caught sight of Omar, the ice-cream seller, who was sitting in a corner with a look of sympathy upon his face.

"I'm sorry about your grandfather," said Omar, and there was a shuffling noise as the rest of the customers swivelled around to stare at him. "We all think well of him. It's a shame he's been taken."

There was some nodding and murmuring.

"I'm sure if any of us knew anything, we'd find a way to tell you," he continued, looking around at the rest of the customers.

There was even more shuffling and murmuring, but

no one else spoke up, and the atmosphere became increasingly awkward.

Pearl came over to Max, her face alight with concern.

"I wish I could help," she said. "But as far as I know, only the Keepers can get into the castle."

Max sat back down, feeling foolish.

Kit had an *I told you so* expression on her face.

"Let's go," he muttered, wanting to get out of the cafe as quickly as possible.

"So what do we do now?" asked Kit, as soon as they were outside. "I need to let my parents know I'm okay – they'll be wondering where I am. I just slipped out earlier without telling them."

"I'm going back to Bram's," said Max. "I want to have another go at spellstopping. At least I'll be doing something."

"Come over if you get lonely," said Kit. "We can try to think of another plan."

Max nodded absent-mindedly. He still felt that him learning how to spellstop was their best hope at present. It seemed unlikely that they would come up with a better idea without any new information.

They said goodbye and went their separate ways – Kit down a side street towards her own home, and Max back along the main street, heading for the road that went in the direction of the farmhouse. Before he'd gone twenty metres from Pearl's cafe, he suddenly felt a horrible drenching sensation. The drying charm that Pearl had cast had worn off and his clothes had returned to their former sodden state. Sea water dripped down his back, and puddled in his shoes. He squelched down the street, trying not to feel discouraged.

But things didn't get better once he'd got home. Max spent the entire afternoon trying and failing to learn how to spellstop, until he finally collapsed into bed, utterly exhausted, but not one bit closer to rescuing Bram.

15

The castle was getting worse. When Max woke up the next morning and looked out of his window, he saw that the green mist was curling like huge vaporous snakes around the castle walls, spreading out across the surrounding water. Dark clouds were gathering above the mass of spiky turrets, and the whole building looked as if it was shuddering very slightly, which gave it an oddly blurry look. Max didn't know what this meant, but it couldn't be good.

Then he caught sight of something else. A plume of black smoke was rising up into the still morning air. It was coming from the village. Max leaned right out of the window, trying to see what it was, but all he could see were the distant roofs and chimney pots.

There was a skidding, crunching noise as Kit appeared on her red bike. She sped through the gates and braked violently.

"Pearl's cafe's burned down!" she cried, catching sight of him as she got off her bike.

Max shot downstairs at once. Kit was already in the kitchen, surrounded by the dogs.

"What happened?" he asked, even though a part of him already knew the answer.

"Leandra appeared a couple of hours after we left," said Kit, who was looking shaken. "She took one look at the cafe and set fire to it."

"Is Pearl hurt? What about the customers – was anyone in there?"

"She's not hurt – just really upset. The owls chased everyone else away."

"Didn't she try to defend herself?" asked Max. "She's a sand witch, after all."

"There's no way her charms would have been any defence against Leandra," said Kit. "They're nowhere near strong enough – it's a completely different sort of magic. But, Max, the cafe's ruined and so is her shop. It's horrible – we helped her put out the fire last night and everything's all charred and burned."

"Do you think it was something to do with what I said?" asked Max, thinking back to his impromptu speech the day before about standing up to the Keeper.

"What if Leandra heard about it?"

"I don't know," said Kit, looking troubled. "She seems to know about everything that happens in the village. I keep telling you – that's why everyone's always hiding away. I can't believe Pearl was brave enough to make a stand."

"Maybe we should go over now – see if there's anything we can do to help."

"Pearl's already left the village," said Kit. "She was too scared to stay in Yowling any longer."

"She's gone?" Max could hardly believe it. "But I thought she had to live near the sea. And her home's here."

"She said she was going to stay with some relatives in Cornwall. To be honest, I'm not sure if she's coming back."

A blazing knot of anger was beginning to flare up in Max. In the space of twenty-four hours, Leandra had taken his grandfather and driven one of the nicest people he'd ever met out of the village.

At that moment, a blue sports car roared into the farmyard and the dogs started barking.

"Ssh," said Kit, trying to calm them.

Max went over to the door. A man with long grey locs climbed out of the car.

"I've come for my painting," he said. "Is Mr Harrow here?"

"No, he's not," said Max shortly.

"But he said I could come and pick it up first thing this morning."

Max wished that the man would just go away. There were more important things to worry about. Kit appeared in the doorway, clinging onto Banana and Sardine – who were still barking – by their collars. Treacle was sitting quietly beside Bram's chair, as if expecting him to return at any moment.

"I think the painting's been mended," she said. "It's in the workshop, just beside the door."

"I'll get it," said Max impatiently, and headed across the yard in his bare feet. The man was gazing at him with a confused expression on his face, and Max suddenly became aware that he was still in his stripy pyjamas. He'd been so distracted by Kit's news that he'd completely forgotten he was wearing them.

He spotted the painting as soon as he set foot in the workshop – it was the portrait of the Victorian gentleman. Bram had carefully rebalanced it, so it now made anyone who looked at it feel pleasantly calm, rather than completely hypnotized. Max avoided making eye contact with it. He didn't want to feel calm – he just wanted to find a way to get to Bram.

"Lovely," said the man, gazing at it, then breaking into a smile.

He reached into his pocket and pulled out a handful of notes.

"We'd settled on four hundred," he said, holding them out to Max.

"Oh," said Max, in surprise. "Right. Er, thanks."

He took the cash and thrust the painting into the man's hands.

"Goodbye, then," he said, and held the workshop door open.

But the man didn't go away. He was still hovering there, as if he was expecting something.

"Er…do you want anything else?"

"A receipt, of course."

Max had no idea what a spellstopping receipt looked like – he had certainly never seen Bram write one. Most of the customers just seemed glad that their precious antiques were no longer trying to kill them. He grabbed a spare bit of paper and wrote *£400 FOR FIXING PAINTING. THANK YOU,* on it. Then, as an afterthought, he signed his name, making it extra squiggly.

"There you go," he said, handing it to the man, praying silently that he would finally go away.

The man looked at it. For a moment it seemed like he was going to insist on something else, but then he just thanked Max, put the painting in his car and drove off, much to Max's relief.

As soon as he had vanished up the lane, Kit came over to Max.

"How did the spellstopping go?" she asked.

"Not good. I spent all of yesterday afternoon trying, but I still can't do it."

"Maybe you were tired," suggested Kit. "After everything that happened at the castle. Why not try again now?"

"All right," said Max.

He glanced over to the long workbench, where the stuffed weasel was sitting, clicking its sharp pointed teeth. He sighed, took a deep breath, and tried to empty his mind, then went over and seized it. A violent surge of magic crackled through him. Max reeled backwards. It felt as if someone had punched him in the chest.

"I don't get what I'm doing wrong," he said angrily, once he'd got his breath back. "I'm doing exactly what Bram said."

"The thing is, Max," said Kit hesitantly, "don't take this the wrong way, but you don't look like your mind's clear at all. Every time you try, you're frowning."

"I'm not!"

"You are – you're doing it right now! It's as if you're worried that something bad is going to happen."

"Well it is!" cried Max. "Bad things happen to me all the time! Either I get bitten, or electrocuted, or I break something, or I kill it. I might as well expect the worst, because it's going to happen anyway."

"Or maybe it keeps happening because you're expecting it to?"

"That's just stupid," said Max. "I'm being realistic."

"No, you're being really annoying," said Kit, sounding thoroughly exasperated. They both glared at each other, on the brink of having an argument, then the dogs started barking again.

"It's probably another customer," said Kit curtly, and she stalked out of the workshop, slamming the door behind her.

Max scowled after her, feeling like he wanted to kick something. Then his irritation slowly began to subside, and he found himself thinking about what Kit had said. Maybe his mind hadn't been that clear, after all. He stared fixedly at a point on the wall and tried not to think of anything. He scrunched his face up, and then relaxed it. He took a deep breath in and let it go. At first, his thoughts kept jumbling around his mind, but he refused to listen to them. He carried on taking deep breaths and staring at the wall, and then, miraculously, they trailed off.

For the first time, Max felt like his brain wasn't actually thinking about anything at all. He was just existing. It was an odd sensation, but a good one. He blinked a couple of times, then slowly looked about the room, his gaze settling on the weasel upon its wooden stand. A murmur of anxiety began to bubble up inside him, but he returned to breathing slowly, in and out, and little by little those thoughts slipped away, leaving his mind free once more.

This time, the weasel didn't bite him when he touched it. Max could feel the energy coursing through him like before, but the difference was that now it didn't hurt him at all. He was just aware of it. What was even more surprising was that he felt as if he could control where the magical energy went. It could either go back the way it came, into the object, or else he could let it seep out in the other direction, to diffuse away. Without consciously thinking about it, he let the magic drain away, into the air. He hadn't even had to take his shoes off.

"You did it?"

Kit had come back, and was staring at him, open-mouthed. Max blinked, as if coming out of a trance, and the usual jumble of thoughts and feelings flooded back into his mind.

"I don't know," he said, and he waved his hand in front of the weasel's face. Normally this was its cue to start gnashing its teeth at him, but it stayed completely still. He picked up the stand and examined it, then ran a hand across its rough fur. There wasn't a trace of magic left in it.

"Yeah," he said slowly. "I think I did."

16

"Come outside," said Kit, once they had got over the surprise of Max learning how to spellstop. "There's someone out there who wants to talk to you."

"Who?"

"A man from the village – I've never spoken to him before, but he says he might know of a way into the castle."

Hope shot through Max as he hurried out of the workshop. A man was pacing about the yard. He was quite small, with a long black beard that reached to his waist and an enormous cream-coloured fisherman's jersey that fell lumpily to his knees. Max recognized him as one of the customers from Pearl's cafe the previous afternoon. When he caught sight of Max, he gave a little jump of alarm, and quickly scanned the sky as if he was afraid that the Keepers would descend on him at any moment. Finding that the coast was clear, he hurried over to them and spoke in a very fast whisper, as if he was scared of being overheard.

"I might know of a way into the castle, but you have to promise not to tell anyone I told you. D'you promise?"

"Yes, of course," said Max at once.

"When you said that stuff about your grandad yesterday I nearly spoke up then, but it was too dangerous. She's got spies everywhere. I don't want no trouble."

"We won't tell anyone," said Kit.

The man looked from Max to Kit then back to Max again and finally nodded.

"I've never been in the castle myself, but the story goes that there's an underground tunnel that goes from the cliffs, right underneath the cove and leads into the castle. My great-grandfather told me about it."

"Where's the entrance?" asked Max, his excitement rising.

"There's supposed to be some sort of cave in the cliffs," said the man, tugging nervously at his long beard. "I've never gone looking for it – I stay well clear of the castle and the Keepers. They give me the collywobbles. But like Omar said, we all like your grandad, and good on you for wanting to rescue him. And if you're a spellstopper, you'll have a better shot at surviving in that place than any of the rest of us."

He was looking at Max with something like respect. Max felt a bit peculiar – he wasn't used to people treating him like that. It occurred to him that Bram must have been quite an important figure in the village, because of his previous connection with the Keepers and keeping the castle under control.

"That's all I have to tell you," concluded the man, as he took another furtive glance at the sky. "I'll be off now. Don't want anyone to know I've been here."

He hurried away, back towards the village, his jumper flapping about his legs, almost tripping him up. Max watched him go, his earlier excitement ebbing a little. He had been expecting something more useful – precise instructions perhaps, or an offer to help them break into the castle. Instead they had just been told a rumour. He turned to Kit, expecting her to be as disappointed as he was, but she was looking completely thunderstruck.

"What's the matter?"

"Max, I think I know where the entrance to that tunnel is."

"Where?" cried Max, in surprise.

"The shell grotto, of course! Why else would

something like that be built in the middle of the cliffs? There's no proper entrance to it, it's completely hidden away – it *must* be something to do with the castle."

Max stared at her. She had a point. If there really was a secret tunnel that led to the castle, that strange cave seemed like the ideal place to conceal it.

"Let's go there now," he said. "We've lost loads of time already. If there really is a tunnel, we need to find it quickly."

"Right," said Kit, snapping into action. "I'll get together some supplies – you get dressed. You're still in your pyjamas."

By the time Max returned, fully dressed, Kit was rummaging around the kitchen, lugging a large canvas holdall that usually lived in the workshop.

"I think that's everything," she said, tossing in a loaf of bread.

"What's in there?" asked Max, peering curiously at the bulging bag.

"This and that," said Kit vaguely. "It's best to be prepared."

The dogs were waiting by the door, clearly keen to come with them.

As Max and Kit left, Sardine squeezed out through the door, swiftly followed by Banana and Treacle. They raced about the yard, happy to be outside. Max felt slightly guilty. Bram always made a point of exercising them twice a day, but Max had been too preoccupied to bring them any further than the farmyard.

"Let's take them with us," he said, not wanting to waste any more time trying to coax them back into the kitchen. "They need a walk."

Kit didn't looked thrilled by the prospect, but she nodded.

"Okay," she said. "I'll leave my bike here though – it won't fit through the rocks and someone might notice if I leave it propped against the cliffs."

They made their way down to the cove. Max was almost running in his eagerness to get there, the dogs bounding along beside him. Kit was weighed down by her heavy bag, but she steadfastly refused any help.

As the cove came into view, Max saw with relief that it was completely deserted. They headed straight for the cliffs, keeping an eye out for any sign of owls. Although Max was looking for the entrance to the grotto, he couldn't find it. For a moment, he wondered if it had simply vanished, like the disappearing castle door.

"It's here," said Kit, and she ducked around what looked like a sheer sheet of rock, to where the gap in the cliff face was concealed. It was easy to see why no one else in Yowling seemed to know about it – you could walk right past and never know it was there.

The dogs did not enjoy going through the narrow slit in the rock face – in fact, they were so upset by the prospect that Max began to seriously regret bringing them. Only Banana – who had always been the most reckless of the trio – could be coaxed into following Kit down the tunnel that led into the cave. Treacle and Sardine simply sat down and refused to budge, so Max had to push them, one at a time, through the dark, damp route into the cave. The dogs were large and extremely reluctant, and his arms were aching by the time Treacle had finally been shoved down the steep slope to join the others. Max almost fell down after her, and collapsed, panting, onto the shell-covered floor of the enormous grotto, his arms across his face to stop the dogs from licking him.

"I've been thinking – since there's no obvious entrance to a tunnel, there must be some sort of concealed door," said Kit, who was already examining the walls. "It makes sense – if you're going to take the trouble to put a castle in the middle of the sea, you don't want just anyone to be able to wander in."

Max got to his feet and joined her. As he looked around the cave, he realized how monumental their task was. The place was enormous. A hidden entrance could be anywhere. The walls were covered in intricate panels that formed a series of archways. Each one was filled with elaborate floral designs made from countless coloured shells.

Kit was running her fingers across the flowers, pressing each one in turn, clearly hoping that she would find the catch to a hidden door. Max tried to look for the outline of an entrance, or some sort of clue that might take them closer to what they were searching for, but there was nothing to suggest where the tunnel might be.

They both worked their way around the perimeter of the cave. The dogs lay down beside the pool, watching them. It took hours. Max became more anxious as time dragged on. He couldn't stop thinking about Bram and what Leandra might be doing to him.

"I give up," said Kit, sounding tired. "This is impossible."

Max didn't reply, even though he secretly agreed with her.

He stepped right back to the edge of the pool and stared around the cave, at the swirling floral patterns that reached right up to the high ceiling. They could search for weeks and never find a hidden door.

And yet as he gazed at the walls, he saw that a shape was slowly emerging from some of the flowers. Suddenly, he saw the huge face of an owl, staring back him. It was made from hundreds of glimmering shells, set into the wall just above their heads, and now that Max had seen it, it seemed unbelievable that he hadn't noticed it before. It seemed to dominate the whole grotto, its huge sightless eyes boring into him.

"Kit!" he called, and pointed.

"What?" she said, looking at the wall in confusion.

"The owl! There!"

Kit frowned. Then her eyes widened and she clapped a hand to her mouth. She got to her feet and they both went over to the giant bird's face. It was as if the atmosphere in the grotto had changed now they had seen it. Before it had seemed strange and wonderful. Now it felt threatening and hostile.

They looked up at it apprehensively. Max's nerves were on edge. All his instincts were screaming at him to get as far away from this place as possible. But instead he reached up his hand and pressed the sharp beak. It sank inwards, with a low rumble, into the rock. Max sprang back, and Kit gasped as the entire archway gave a shudder. A door swung open. It was made of a thick slab of solid stone but seemed to open as easily as if it was on hinges.

Max looked into the passage beyond. They had found the tunnel.

17

Max stepped forwards, into the blackness. The tunnel smelled odd – it had the same damp sea-salt tang as the grotto, but mixed with something else, a putrid reek that reminded Max of rotten meat. He strained his eyes to see, but then a beam of torchlight drove back the dark.

"I brought one for you too," said Kit, passing him a torch.

Max hadn't realized that Bram owned one torch, let alone two. He felt a wave of gratitude towards Kit – she really was extremely organized, no matter what the situation.

Apprehensive about what lay ahead, Max flicked the switch of his torch. It promptly electrocuted him, then broke.

"Ouch!" he cried, dropping it. The torch rolled away,

and the dogs, who had followed them through the archway, started sniffing it.

Kit shone her torch at him, and he could see the dismay in her eyes.

"I thought you were okay with electricity now," she said.

Max shrugged defensively. "I wasn't concentrating."

As he spoke, a familiar wave of despair hit him. Ever since he'd figured out how to spellstop, he'd thought all his problems on that front were over. Clearly they weren't.

"It's okay," said Kit, trying to make the best of it. "We've still got my torch."

The bright yellow beam bounced off the wet, black rock, as they made their way down a passage that got gradually smaller and smaller the further along they went. It felt very old, as if it had been made many centuries ago, and the ground was rough and covered with rubble that crunched and slid underneath their feet. They had only been walking for a few minutes when the tunnel came to an abrupt stop, blocked by an enormous heap of rocks.

"Do you know what's weird?" said Kit, examining the wall. "Someone has bricked it up deliberately. You can see from the way the rocks have been piled on top of each other."

"It was probably Leandra, or one of the Keepers before her," suggested Max. "I bet they did it to stop anyone getting into the castle."

"I just hope that we can clear it," said Kit. "If we can pull a few out, we should be able to climb through."

Max was beginning to feel peculiar. He wasn't sure why. It was as if all his skin was prickling. It was a bit like the feeling he got when he was about to touch something that had electricity in it. He wondered if it was just the after-effects of being shocked by the torch.

Meanwhile, Kit had dug her fingers into the edge of one of the stones and was pulling at it. With a loud *thunk*, it fell out of the wall and landed on the ground. Banana gave a yelp of surprise and shot behind the other two dogs.

"One down," said Kit triumphantly, and Max pulled himself together and stepped forwards to join in.

It was gruelling work. Each rock seemed to weigh a tonne, and they were stacked so closely together that it was difficult to get a good grip on them. It was made harder by the fact that they only had the one torch, and they kept having to balance it on bits of rock so that their hands were free. Soon, Max felt the same odd, prickling feeling again.

"Do you feel anything?" he asked Kit. "Like there's electricity in the air?"

"No," replied Kit, frowning at him. "Is something the matter? You look weird."

"It's nothing," said Max quickly, and he shook his head, trying to rid himself of the unsettling sensation. They were in an eerie dark tunnel, about to go under the sea. Of course it would feel a bit strange.

They had only moved a few more stones when they struck a weak point, and the entire wall tumbled down. Max and Kit sprang aside, pressing themselves against the side of the passage to stay out of the way. When the rocks had settled, there was enough room for them and the dogs to easily climb through. They scrambled over the mound of rubble, then carried on along the tunnel. Soon, it began to slope steeply downwards.

"We must be going under the sea," said Kit. There was barely enough room now for them to walk side by side. Max was getting the prickling feeling again. It was made worse by knowing that they were going underneath the cove, that there was a whole body of water pressing down on top of him. It wasn't just that though – the stale, thin air still felt like it was crackling with energy. If anything, it was getting stronger. He had never encountered anything like it before. In his experience, electricity was always connected to an object or a particular point. This seemed to be all around him.

He wondered if the energy could shock him even though he wasn't able to touch it – it seemed unlikely, but he tried his best to stay as calm as possible, as if he was about to turn on a light switch or spellstop something. There was no point in taking any risks.

"Max," whispered Kit, her voice breaking in on his thoughts. She had stopped dead and looked scared. "I think there's something coming towards us."

Max stopped and listened. There was a funny sort of scuffling, rattling noise echoing through the tunnel. Someone or something was clattering over the uneven floor ahead of them. He scrunched up his eyes, trying to see beyond the thin beam of torchlight, into the dark. The sound was getting louder – a dragging, crunching series of thumps. All three dogs started growling.

Kit and Max stood frozen, not knowing if they should meet whatever it was head on, or if they should turn and run. The tunnel felt smaller and more stifling than ever.

The shuffling noise grew louder.

Then, out of the darkness came a huge lizard-like creature with thick leathery skin and a blunt nose. It looked like a cross between a dragon and a dinosaur and it filled up the whole of the tunnel. It had a thickset body and its forelegs ended in big, sharp claws, which made a harsh scraping noise as it padded forwards across the uneven rock.

It paused, blinking in the light for a moment, then it spotted them. It let out a hoarse rattling hiss that echoed eerily around the confined space, and its long, forked tongue flicked angrily as it propelled itself towards them. The dogs yelped and fled back along the tunnel, and Max and Kit wasted no time in following close behind.

They could hear the creature chasing after them. Even though they were running as fast as they could, it was clear that it was gaining ground.

"It's no use," gasped Kit. "We won't get out in time."

She grabbed a rock and hurled it at the creature. It roared furiously but stopped in its tracks.

Max yelled at the top of his voice, hoping to scare it off. The creature hissed back at them and tried to rear up on its hind legs. Its great head struck the roof of the tunnel and its enormous tail thrashed at the sides, beating the rock with great juddering blows.

Max wondered if this was it – if he was going to die. Kit had seized another stone to hurl at the beast, but Max was frozen to the spot. The energy in the tunnel felt as if it was pulsing through him, mirroring the beating of his own heart. It was the same feeling he got when he was spellstopping, but it felt bigger and stranger than when he'd spellstopped the stuffed weasel. For a moment, he let the unfamiliar energy swirl around inside him, feeling it crackle and dance through his body like millions of tiny lightning bolts, and then he let it go. It seemed to seep out of him, slowly draining away to nothing. As soon as it was over, Max could tell that the atmosphere in the tunnel had changed, even though the huge lizard was still roaring furiously, just a couple of metres away.

However, this time, as it thrashed about, something began to happen. As it struck the roof of the tunnel, a shower of stones rattled down and large cracks splintered across the walls.

"Run!" yelled Max.

They turned and fled. The dogs had already bolted, back along the passage towards the grotto. There was a huge deafening rumble behind them as the roof caved in and the tunnel began to collapse. Rock came raining downwards, along with a heap of rubble and sand, swiftly followed by a huge torrent of water. The good thing was that it created a barrier between them and the enormous lizard, but the downside was that the tunnel was now rapidly filling up with sea water. Max was running for his life, but even through his fear, he felt a fierce wave of disappointment. The tunnel – their only way of reaching Bram – was ruined. The water kept surging up towards them, but because of the sharp gradient, they were able to remain above it, as long as they didn't slow down.

"Are you okay?" Max called, glancing over his shoulder at Kit.

"Yes!" she panted. "We've got to keep going – we're not high enough yet."

Max was gasping painfully for breath, his heart racing, but he forced himself to carry on running uphill. It felt like the end was almost in sight when the passage finally levelled off and they scrambled over the mound of rocks that they had cleared only a short time before. The water seemed to have slowed – they were well above it now – so it was not quite as bad as it could have been when Kit's torch flickered and went out, and they were plunged into darkness.

"We must be nearly there," she panted.

Max's lungs were hurting so much that he wasn't able to reply. They carried on along the passage, their hands outstretched like zombies, feeling their way, as they stumbled on the uneven ground and groped blindly forwards into the blackness. It felt like an eternity, but at last they spotted a small patch of pale grey light up in front of them. It was the archway back into the shell grotto. They kept going, not daring to relax until they were out of the tunnel and had heaved the heavy stone door shut.

Kit collapsed onto the ground, too exhausted to stand any longer. The dogs followed suit, panting heavily. Max sat down next to them, his heart still pounding. For several long minutes, they didn't say a word.

"We're lucky to have got out of there alive," said Kit eventually, sitting up and clasping her arms around her knees. "What was that thing?"

"No idea," replied Max. "But there was something strange about that tunnel. I think I must have spellstopped something in there, just before the roof caved in."

"What do you mean? Was it something to do with that monster?"

"I don't think so. It was like it was something in the

air. I can't explain it. I've never come across a place that felt like that before."

Kit looked as puzzled as Max felt.

"It doesn't matter though, does it?" added Max, as the awfulness of their situation really began to sink in. "The tunnel's destroyed. How are we supposed to get to Bram now?"

"I don't know," said Kit. She sounded tired and defeated, and had a cut on the side of her face. "There's thirteen owls all keeping a lookout – and that's not even including Leandra. No matter what we try, they'll be expecting us."

"But we have to do something," said Max.

Kit didn't answer. Max knew what she was thinking. What if they weren't able to rescue Bram after all?

18

It was hard, being completely out of ideas. Max felt like his best chance of spotting an opportunity was to keep a close eye on the castle. This was why, the morning after their escape from the tunnel, he was sitting on his bedroom windowsill, surveying Yowling Castle through a pair of binoculars. Things were getting even more alarming over there. One of the towers had collapsed, and the owls were wheeling in tight circles above the broken masonry. The green mist and the dark clouds had spread right across the cove and had almost reached the village, giving the whole place an eerie feeling, as if something very bad was about to happen.

Max wondered what was going on. Was the castle starting to fall apart of its own accord or was it something to do with Bram? Or could the castle's sudden decline be linked to what had happened in the tunnel the day before?

He was deep in thought when Sardine started howling, and he realized that somebody was knocking on the front door of the farmhouse. Max hurried down the stairs and found a small, nervous-looking woman standing on the doorstep, clasping what looked like a jewellery box. It was another customer. Before Max could tell her to go away, she started talking, very quickly.

"It's been in my family for generations," she began, clearly distressed. "I inherited it from my grandmother. I thought I was losing my mind at first, until I realized that it was the necklace. Now I never put it on. I didn't know what to do, but then my friend showed me a painting that you'd fixed. I thought that maybe you'd be able to help…"

She trailed off, looking pleadingly at Max.

"I can't help, I'm afraid," said Max. "I'm too busy."

"Please!" she cried, looking as if she was about to burst into tears. "This is my last hope."

Max relented.

"What exactly is wrong with it?" he asked, looking warily at the box.

"It makes you forget everything as soon as you put it on," she said in a rush, looking even more anxious than before. She snapped the box open to reveal a glittering diamond necklace.

"And what was it supposed to do?" asked Max. "What was its power to start with?"

"To start with?" The woman looked confused. "I don't want it to have any powers!" she burst out. "I just want it to be an ordinary necklace!"

Max was suddenly a lot more interested. He had spent the previous evening working on all the enchanted objects that had been left in Bram's workshop – the sapphire ring, the cursed cup, and even a set of toy soldiers that had developed unpleasantly murderous tendencies. Everything Bram had taken on required rebalancing the object, not removing the magic completely. This was an opportunity to spellstop something stronger than a stuffed weasel.

"I'm sure I can fix it," he said eagerly. "Leave it with me."

The woman hesitated.

"Would you mind if I waited?" she asked. "Only because it's so valuable I'm frightened to let it out of my sight. It's worth more than my house."

"All right," said Max, taking the box. "I'll do it now."

"Can I watch you mend it?" she asked, following him over to the workshop.

"No!" said Max quickly. The idea of her staring at him

while he experimented with spellstopping was not an appealing prospect. "You can wait here though," he added. "It shouldn't take too long."

"That's fine," she said hastily, her face flushing with embarrassment. "It's a lovely day. I do appreciate you letting me wait."

Max went into the workshop, leaving her wandering about the yard, calling to the chickens. For a moment he wondered if he should have locked the kitchen door, but she looked so harmless that it seemed silly to worry.

He put the jewellery box down on the workbench and opened it up. The rows of diamonds glimmered up at him, catching the light. He lifted the necklace up and felt a familiar feeling crackle through his fingertips. He could tell that it was full of magic. Not long ago, he wouldn't have been able to hold a necklace like this without it hurting him. Now, it was easy. Max was so absorbed in what he was doing that he didn't even notice a large dark owl had silently swooped down and was perched on the windowsill, looking in at him. Instead, he ran the necklace through his fingers, closed his eyes and got to work.

He soon reached the point at which he would usually have stopped – when the magic felt contained in the necklace, instead of sparking outwards as it had done to start with. But this time, he kept going, forcing the magic to keep draining away. The necklace starting shaking in his hands, almost as if it was a living thing. He could feel it resisting him, fighting back, but then suddenly all the energy seemed to flow out of it and he was left clutching a completely inert piece of jewellery. He opened his eyes and examined it. There wasn't the slightest trace of magic left. Max beamed broadly. He'd done it.

"AAAAARGH!"

A blood-curdling scream ripped through the air. Max dropped the necklace back into its box and dashed outside, just in time to see its owner driving away at full speed, the wheels of her car sending gravel and dirt spitting up in her wake.

"Hey!" yelled Max, waving his arms after the car. "You left your necklace!"

Then he stopped dead. Leandra was standing beside the workshop. There were dark rings under her eyes and her face had a bloodless quality, her skin tinged almost green, as if the castle's worsening state was affecting her too. But she still seemed as pleased with herself as ever.

"I think I scared away your customer," she said, her dark eyes glinting with amusement. "Oops."

"What did you do to her?" demanded Max.

Leandra just smiled and shook her head, as if she couldn't possibly say.

"You've learned how to spellstop," she said eventually. "I saw you through the window."

"So what if I have? Where's Bram? Is he still alive?"

"Bram is absolutely fine."

"When are you going to let him go?"

"He can leave as soon as he fixes the castle," snapped Leandra, her mood changing at once. "All I want is to keep Yowling Castle from falling down. Previously, that's been quite easy, as there's always been a spellstopper willing to step in. But your grandfather would rather see the castle collapse than lift a finger to help."

"He can't!" retorted Max. "How many times do you need to be told that?"

Leandra scowled at him, looking so annoyed that Max wondered if she was going to attack him. But she didn't.

"I think you should come with me to the castle," she said instead. "If you can spellstop, you'll be able to help him."

Max opened his mouth to refuse, then closed it again. This was his opportunity – a way into the castle.

Once he'd found Bram, made sure that he was okay, then surely the two of them would be able to find a way out. If not, perhaps he really could help his grandfather with the spellstopping and then Leandra would let them both go.

"All right."

Leandra's bad mood immediately lifted. She gave a wide smile, showing her white teeth.

"Perfect," she said.

"As long as you promise to release us if we can't fix the castle."

Leandra just laughed and shook her head. She cupped her hands together, raised them to her mouth, and blew into them, making a long low whistle that sounded just like the hooting call of an owl. Max heard a series of answering cries and the entire flock of Keepers came swooping down through the sky towards them.

"It's best not to wriggle," said Leandra. "That way, there's less chance of them dropping you."

"That's how we're getting to the castle?" asked Max, who was suddenly having serious second thoughts.

"No," said Leandra. "That's how *you're* getting there. I can fly by myself."

"Isn't there another way…?" he began, but the owls

were already closing in on him. He felt them seize hold of his jumper and his arms, and their gnarled talons clasped around his wrists. One of them even grabbed hold of his hair, which made his eyes water. Then the owls started to flap their wings, all at once, and Max felt their grip on him tighten as they began to rise up. His feet left the ground and all of a sudden he was kicking at the empty air.

It was the most terrifying experience of his life, except for possibly the incident in the tunnel. He couldn't even see properly. There were so many birds clustered around him that his view kept getting obscured by their beating wings, which fanned his face so strongly that it felt like he was in the middle of a storm. He could only see where they were going in snatches – he caught a glimpse of the beach, far below him, then a brief flash of the rippling waves. His jumper was digging painfully into his armpits, his scalp was aching and he felt as if he was in constant danger of plummeting fatally downwards.

Soon, he could see the black towers of the castle beneath him, and then they were swooping swiftly down towards it. The owls all released him at once, and Max landed heavily on the flat roof at the centre of the circle of towers, lost his balance and fell to his knees.

For a moment he kneeled there, still hardly able to believe he'd survived the flight. The owls went back to wheeling around in the sky overhead, as if nothing had happened. He glanced over the low wall that ran round the edge of the roof and felt sick at the dizzying drop to the rocks below.

"How was the journey?"

Leandra came towards him, her long black hair whipping about her in the wind. Something was glinting around her neck.

"You took the necklace!" cried Max indignantly.

"I can take whatever I like," she said, smiling nastily at him. "I do whatever I want. You really should be more frightened of me, Max."

She flicked her finger at him and a burst of flame shot towards him, stopping in mid-air just before it touched his face. He could feel the heat of it as he stumbled backwards, away from her.

Leandra closed her fist and the fire vanished at once.

"Don't worry. I won't kill you. Not yet, anyway."

Max tried his best not to look scared.

"Where's Bram?" he asked, wanting to see his grandfather more than anything.

Leandra shrugged. "I have no idea."

"What do you mean?" said Max, his voice rising in alarm. "Where are you keeping him?"

"Max," she said, with a dramatic sigh. "Look around you. Look at the size of this castle. Your grandfather could be anywhere."

Max looked at her uncertainly. He wasn't sure if she was playing some sort of horrible game with him.

"Do you think I've shut him up in a dungeon?" she said lightly. "Locked him up in a room, with nothing but bread and water? Of course I haven't. I don't need to. He's free to go about the castle as he chooses. Hopefully he might decide to fix it, but as yet, he hasn't shown any signs of doing so."

"So I can just go and look for him?" asked Max suspiciously.

"Yes, of course. I think it's better if you speak to him alone first, without me being there. He seems to have taken against me," she said, making a face. "He won't listen to anything I say. Maybe you'll be able to make him see sense."

Max glanced around, his eyes settling on a door that was set into the nearest tower.

"Go," said Leandra, gesturing. "I'll be back later."

As he turned away from her, he heard a whoosh and

the sound of beating wings. When he glanced up, he saw that she had turned back into an owl and was flying away, the glint of the diamond necklace twinkling around her feathered neck.

19

It was only after Leandra had gone and Max was left alone on the roof that the reality of his situation really began to sink in. Now that he had finally arrived at the castle, he realized the sheer scale of what he had got himself into. The castle was enormous – the vast flat roof stretched out in all directions, with the soaring dark towers rising up around the edges. The ominous clouds that had gathered above the castle blocked the sunlight, making it feel even more eerie and oppressive. Although Max was just on the roof, he could already tell that the building was in an even worse state than he had imagined. The slates had slid off the sharply pointed roofs of the towers, and parts of the walls had collapsed, leaving gaping black holes. The outside of the building was completely covered in a dark slimy moss – Max could feel it squelching damply every time he took a step. But the most unsettling thing of all was the way that the entire castle was shuddering very slightly. Max had never experienced an earthquake, but he imagined that this was what the beginning of one would feel like.

He went over to the door that he had spotted, set into the side of one of the towers. He hesitated for a moment before he touched the handle, but it turned when he opened it. He'd been wondering whether he would have problems with the castle, given his sensitivity to different forms of energy. But it seemed as if the magic that governed Yowling Castle was a more complex sort than anything he had previously encountered – it felt bigger, somehow, and older, as if it was too important to be affected by someone as small as him.

Still feeling apprehensive, Max made his way down a flight of steps and came out into a long corridor festooned with cobwebs. As he made his way along it, a floorboard vanished just as he was about to step onto it. He stopped dead, and peered down through the hole to the floor far below. His heart was thudding in alarm, but he took a deep breath and forced himself to jump over the gap. A couple of steps later, the same thing happened again, but this time Max's foot was actually on the board. His leg plunged downwards, and Max lurched forwards away from the jagged hole, barely making it to safety. As he recovered from the shock, he spotted a pair of shadows on the wall and for a moment he thought there were some people there, watching him.

"Hello?" he called, and looked around in all directions, but nobody was there.

Max hurried down the rest of the corridor as quickly as he could, and then down another staircase.

He was almost at the bottom when the stairs disappeared from beneath him, and it was lucky that Max managed to grab hold of the handrail. He swung in the air for a moment, then dropped the remaining distance onto the cold stone floor.

He was in a big hallway, with high arched doorways and narrow slit windows that let in very little light. It was echoingly empty and water dripped down the bare walls.

Max went into room after room, and after a while he began to lose track of where he'd been. Each room looked the same, all equally sparse and cold. Again, he saw a strange shadow, flitting along the wall, but there was nobody about. There was an odd humming noise too, like a tuning fork vibrating, which drummed into his head. He couldn't work out where it was coming from –

it seemed to be all around him. It was the sort of noise that would become unbearable if you listened to it for too long.

He went up another staircase, keeping a firm hold on the handrail in case it suddenly vanished, and found himself in a completely circular room with a bed in the centre. It was a simple metal one with a sad, sagging mattress and a few threadbare blankets, but it was still the first bit of furniture that Max had seen. He carried on up the stairs and came out into another room, identical to the one below, except that it had been set up as a sitting room, with a couple of armchairs and a grate filled with ash from a fire. Before he could get a proper look at it, the door slammed behind him and somebody grabbed him by the arm.

"Max," said a hoarse voice.

It was Bram.

He looked terrible. His face was sunken with worry and he stared at Max as if he couldn't believe he was really there.

"You should have stayed away," he croaked. "Did she force you to come?"

"Not exactly," said Max. "I agreed to – I was really worried about you. Now I'm here we can find a way out.

Or I can help you with the spellstopping. Then we can both go home."

"You must've seen something of the castle by now," said Bram, sounding distressed. "It's too big, and the magic's too unbalanced."

"But if both of us tried to do it…"

Max trailed off as he saw the weary expression on his grandfather's face.

"Max, when I spellstopped the castle the first time, it was in a much better state. There was none of this green mist, and bits of it weren't vanishing. And it was almost too much for me even then."

"But there has to be something we can do," said Max. "I've learned how to spellstop – I can help you."

For a moment, Bram's face lit up and he looked at Max with pride, before his expression clouded over once more.

"You've done very well, Max, but it's not going to be any use, I'm afraid. Two spellstoppers can't work on the same thing at once. It's impossible. Magic can only be conducted through one person at a time. Anyway, fixing the castle won't be a permanent solution. The castle's magic is going sour – it's getting more and more unstable. Even if I managed to repair it somehow, the effects wouldn't last as long as they did in my grandmother's day. Might only be a couple of years before the castle needs more work. Then what?"

"It'll have to be done again?" suggested Max.

"Exactly," said Bram. "And who will the Keepers call on once I'm not around? You. It might still be Leandra, or it might be whoever comes after her, but there will be a Keeper and they will come after you. And say that, by some miracle, you do succeed in fixing the castle, then you'll just need to do the same thing again and again, and the task will become harder and harder, and happen more and more often, until eventually it'll kill you too."

"I didn't realize," said Max, stumbling over his words as the enormity of it hit him.

"Course you didn't," said Bram. "But that's why you shouldn't have come. I was all set to go down with the castle – just to put an end to it all."

Bram sank onto the broken chair, looking more miserable than Max had ever seen him before. Max went over to the window and looked out across the waves. It was the same window that he had seen Bram lean out of when he and Kit had embarked on their disastrous rescue mission.

From here, he could see the great jagged rocks that divided the bay from the open sea on one side of him, sticking out of the water like a set of gigantic broken teeth. He could see the vast expanse of deep water that separated the castle from the shore, and the dense green mist that swirled around beneath him, making the distance between the window and the water look even more terrifying.

He turned to his grandfather.

"Is there really no way out?" he asked, his voice betraying how scared he was.

"'Fraid not."

"But the castle's huge," Max persisted. "There could be a door or a window that we've missed. And Leandra's on her own in here – the owls don't come inside, do they? That makes it two of us and one of her. We've got an advantage."

"It's not just Leandra," said Bram grimly. "There's the shadow people."

"The what?"

"When you found your way here, through the castle, you must have noticed them. Strange shadows that move on their own."

"Yes, but I didn't think there was anyone there," said

Max, gazing at Bram in horror. "I thought Leandra was the only person in the castle."

"She is," said Bram. "Shadow people aren't like humans or the magical beings you see in Yowling. They don't have personalities or souls – they're not even like ghosts. They're just a sort of shadow that functions like a person in some ways – they can take orders, they're even able to move things about. They're part of the castle's magic – they only obey the Keeper. So you don't want to cross them. And they're everywhere."

Max shivered, despite himself. He glanced around the room, his eyes resting on any suspicious-looking shadows. He understood, now, why Bram looked so exhausted and drawn. It was impossible to relax for a moment when you knew you were being watched.

"Look, Max, escaping this place is impossible. I never wanted you to get mixed up in all this. I'm going to think of a way to get you out."

"Get *us* out," corrected Max. "What if there's another tunnel out of here? Kit and I found one, but I made it collapse, so we'd have to try another way."

"What tunnel?" asked Bram, and Max told him what had happened in the tunnel under the sea.

"You must have come across a ley line," said Bram.

"Sometimes you get very faint electrical currents that run through the earth, and that tunnel must've been built along one of them. Makes sense, now I think about it – there's probably a few of them underneath the castle. You often get strange things built on top of ley lines."

"Well, it's gone now," said Max. "I spellstopped it."

"You what?" Bram seemed surprised.

"I just…stopped it. The same way I'd spellstop anything. That was when the tunnel caved in."

"But that's remarkable! I've never heard of anything like it. No wonder the castle's getting so much worse. You must have weakened it. You spellstopped that ley line yesterday afternoon, didn't you? That was the same time the north-west tower collapsed."

Excitement gripped Max.

"What if I tried to spellstop the castle?" he asked urgently. "Not fix it like Leandra wants – maybe I could take away the magic completely?"

"No," said Bram flatly, cutting him off. "No way are you going to try. I've told you before, spellstopping the castle is impossible. It's far too powerful."

"What if we looked for another ley line then? You said the castle's probably built on a few of them – what if we found the others? I could spellstop them, and that might wreck the castle for us."

"Not a hope," said Bram, shaking his head. "Those currents are deep underground – you were just lucky that you stumbled across one in the tunnel. You'd never be able to do that again."

The sun had been setting as they were speaking, and shadows started slipping through the crack beneath the door. Bram stopped talking as several shadow people ranged themselves around the walls, flickering about them.

"What's happening?" asked Max.

"Dinner time," said Bram. "No choice – we've got to go. Otherwise they'll drag us there."

Feeling more uncomfortable than ever, Max followed Bram back down the winding stone steps out of their tower. Several of the shadow people followed them, two flitting along the walls and one looming behind them, so there was no way they could turn back.

"Where are we going?" he asked curiously.

"The dining hall," replied Bram. "Leandra will be there. Usually that's when she tries to make me spellstop the castle."

As they went along the empty passageways, Bram pointed out the vanishing floorboards to Max.

"Tends to be the same ones each time," he said. "New ones pop up, but for the most part you can avoid them."

It would have been too dark to see, but someone had lit a few candles which hung in brackets upon the walls, casting a flickering light around the chilly castle. There were more shadows than ever. Some were as big as houses, casting long, looming shapes across the walls. By the time they emerged into a cavernous stone hall, it almost felt like the shadows were whispering as they spun and twisted through the air. The light was stronger here, thanks to a vast iron chandelier that was studded with dozens of tapers that dripped wax down onto the floor below. All the wax had formed into a huge shapeless mound, like a twisted sculpture. It must have taken decades, if not centuries, to form. Max shivered as the shadow people rustled around him.

"They like candlelight," said Bram. "Makes them stronger."

He pushed open a big studded wooden door, and Max followed him inside. Like the rest of the castle, the dining hall was a high, gaunt stone room. A big table stood in the centre with wrought-iron chairs arranged along each side. There was an enormous stone fireplace, which had a small fire crackling in it. As the room was still extremely cold, Max suspected that the meagre fire was for the benefit of the shadow people, as the room was alive with them. There were dozens of them, darting about everywhere. The overall effect was grim: Max couldn't decide if it looked more like a dungeon or an abandoned cathedral. Either way, it was extremely creepy.

Leandra was waiting for them, sitting at the head of the table. She was wearing a different dress – a short black one that floated about her in a cloud of chiffon. She stood up to greet them.

"So you've reunited," she said. "Grandfather and grandson. You must be pleased to see each other."

Bram scowled at Leandra and sat down in a chair that was as far away from her as possible. Max sat down beside him.

"Fine," said Leandra. "Be like that."

She clapped her hands. A door at the side of the room suddenly flew open and a great mass of shadows swirled out of it. At first, Max thought that they were coming to get him and Bram, but then he realized that they were carrying plates of food, which were bobbing along in mid-air towards them.

There was a roast chicken, with roasted potatoes dotted around it, a plate of fat purple plums and a dish of what looked like cooked seaweed. Each of them came to a halt in the middle of the table, just in front of Max and Bram.

"See," said Leandra to Max, as she gestured at the plates. "I've been treating him very well. Go ahead, help yourselves."

Bram immediately began to carve up the chicken and dole it out onto his and Max's plates.

"Eat as much as you can," he hissed at Max. "You don't know when you'll get another chance."

Leandra wasn't eating anything. Instead, she put her elbows on the table and rested her chin in her hands, watching them.

"Did you speak to him, Max?" she asked pleasantly.

"He did," snapped Bram. "I'm still not going to help you."

Leandra rolled her eyes.

"You really are a very annoying old man," she said. "You're lucky I haven't lost patience with you yet."

"That's because you want something," said Bram.

"Yes," said Leandra simply. "And the longer you keep me waiting, the worse the castle gets. But I have an idea."

Before she could continue, she was interrupted by a series of loud crashes somewhere close by. She frowned and made a gesture at the shadow people, who glided rapidly out of the room in the direction of the noise.

Somebody was yelling and Max felt a horrible chill come over him. He knew that voice. A moment later, what looked like a black whirling tornado came into the room and halted beside the table. Then the shadow people drew away, leaving Kit standing there.

"You're alive!" she cried when she saw Max and Bram, then she stopped suddenly as another shadow wrapped around her from head to toe, like a blanket.

Max and Bram both leaped up to go over to her, but shadowy fingers forced them back down into their seats.

Several of the shadow people had glided over to Leandra, and she listened to them as if they were speaking, though Max couldn't hear anything, no matter how hard he tried.

"It sounds like she was found climbing out of a sewage pipe," said Leandra, making a face at the other two. "How unpleasant."

She made a sweeping gesture with her hand and the shadow unwrapped Kit, who glared at Leandra with absolute loathing.

"It's useful, in a way, that you came," continued Leandra, as Kit stared at Max in shock. "Three hostages are better than two."

"Let Max and Kit go," began Bram. "I'll not consider anything until you take them back."

In response, Leandra stabbed her finger at the table and the food in front of them burst into flames.

"I'm not bargaining with you," she said coldly. "And I'm not stupid. It's more useful keeping them here."

She paused and they all stared at her, like rabbits caught in the glare of car headlights.

"Let me make this very simple for you," she said at last. "Either you fix the castle tonight, or one of you will die. And the rest of the Keepers will make sure that there isn't anything left afterwards. I haven't decided yet what order I'll kill you in."

There was a long, horrible pause as Leandra studied them.

"Her first, I think."

She pointed at Kit, who flinched as a blast of flame narrowly missed her ear.

"Then the boy," she continued, and Max ducked as another blast went over his head.

"And finally you."

She pointed her finger at Bram, who didn't duck, or flinch, and Leandra froze as a flame danced at the end of her fingertip. There was a long, horrible moment as they all stared at her, and then she closed her fist, extinguishing the flame.

"I'm not bluffing, old man," she said coolly. "You can't just sit here and wait for the castle to collapse. I'll kill both of them. After that, if you still haven't budged, I'll destroy every single person in Yowling too. I won't stop until you help me."

All Max could smell was the acrid reek of burning food. The plums had turned to ash, the chicken carcass was black and brittle, and the potatoes were lumps of charcoal. The seaweed smelled worst of all, a dish of black powder with a sour vegetable reek.

"It looks like dinner is over," said Leandra, sitting back in her chair.

Max got to his feet and dashed over to Kit. Bram got up slowly, as if he was utterly exhausted.

"Remember," said Leandra, as they left. "You've got until tomorrow morning. If the castle hasn't been fixed by the time the sun rises, that's the end."

20

"Go back to the tower," said Bram, as soon as they had left the dining hall, still reeling from the shock of what had just happened. "I'll see you up there."

"Why?" asked Max at once.

"Got to check something. It's better if I go on my own."

"We're coming with you," said Max.

"You'll be safer in the tower room," insisted Bram.

"I don't think any of us are safe, wherever we are," said Kit, who was looking very pale.

"Tell us what you're planning," said Max. "Whatever you do is going to affect all of us. We're in this together now."

Bram closed his eyes for a moment, as if he couldn't quite cope with the way things were turning out. Then he sighed.

"All right then," he said. "Follow me."

"How did you get into the castle?" Max asked Kit, as they followed Bram down an echoing stone passageway. He spoke in a low voice, aware of the listening shapes that flitted alongside them, blotting out their own shadows.

"It turns out I'm actually a selkie after all," Kit whispered back. "When I saw all the owls dragging you off across the cove, I was so worried that I waded out into the sea after you, and then suddenly I transformed. It was the strangest thing – I didn't know what had happened to begin with. And then I was able to swim over – it hardly took me any time at all."

"Kit, that's amazing news!" exclaimed Max. He knew how much she had minded not being able to transform like her sister.

"Well, it would have been amazing, if I hadn't been caught," she said.

"But how did you get in? Did you get through the mist?"

Kit shook her head.

"I swam round the base of the castle and noticed that there was a drainage channel, so I went up it, then as soon as I was out of the water, I was just somehow able to transform back. I don't know how I did it – I was still wearing the same clothes and I was completely dry. It was really weird. Anyway, once I'd done that I was able to climb up the pipe and into the castle. It was that stupid metal cover that gave me away – it made a really loud rattling noise and those horrible shadowy things caught me. I thought I had a chance at rescuing you, but now we're probably all going to end up dead."

They had been talking louder than they had realized, because Bram suddenly wheeled around.

"Neither of you are going to die if I've got anything to do with it," he said firmly. "Just follow me and keep your wits about you. This castle's dangerous. I've been here before, remember?"

He led them through rooms that were covered in ice and others that were boiling hot and filled with steam. In some places, chunks of the thick stone wall were missing, offering a terrifying view of the sheer drop down to the waves below. They were heading right into the middle part of the castle, down dark corridors that had no windows. But wherever they went, Max could see the shadow people, following their every step.

Finally, Bram stopped at a heavy wooden door, with big iron hinges.

"Don't touch anything," he said. "And whatever you do, stick to the edges of the room."

Max nodded, and so did Kit. Then Bram turned the handle and they all went inside.

"Stay near the walls," warned Bram again, and held out his arms to stop them from going too far in. "This is the heart of the castle – it's where all the magic comes from. One wrong move and you'll be frazzled."

The room was completely circular, and completely empty. It had the same bare stone walls as the rest of the castle and a high vaulted ceiling. The difference was the floor. It was like no floor that Max had ever seen. Aside from a band of plain grey stone running around the edge, it was covered in a huge circular mosaic of coloured marble. Delicate geometric patterns of circles and symbols radiated outwards from a large rock, the colour of opal, that protruded up from the central point. This rock constantly changed colour as Max looked at it, but the heart of it flickered a deep red, as if it was full of flames. The place seemed to crackle with energy and although there were no lights upon the walls, the room glowed. The shadow people hadn't followed them in here. Bram was staring at the rock intently, as if it was telling him something. Max instinctively moved a step closer, to get a better view, but his grandfather turned on him at once.

"Don't touch the floor!" Bram warned him. "There's more energy in here than in a million cars. That stone in the middle is the source of all the magic – it radiates out across the floor and through the whole castle. See that deep red colour? That's a bad sign – it's even further gone than it was last time."

"So you definitely can't fix it?" asked Max.

"No," said Bram. "It'll kill me, but I'm going to try anyway."

"What?" cried Max, while Kit gasped in shock.

"It's the only way. She'll kill you two otherwise."

Max and Kit both started protesting at the same time, but Bram cut them off.

"No point disagreeing. My mind's made up. But you two need to get out of here right now. I don't trust her to let you go – when I fail, I reckon she'll force you to try to fix the castle, Max, and use Kit as a hostage. You can't risk it – it's too dangerous. So here's what you'll do. I'm going to go out there and start shouting for Leandra – I'll tell her I'll do what she wants. That ought to distract the shadows – they'll be so busy watching me, it should give you two a chance to slip away. I'll head off in the other direction, so you can have a clear run at getting back downstairs. Kit, can you get yourself and Max back out the same way you came in?"

"I think so," said Kit. "But…"

"Then leave that way," Bram said. "Help Max once you're in the water, get him back to the shore. Then hide somewhere until you know what's happening with the castle. Your family should hide too. Max, you'll need to leave Yowling. Tell your mother what's happened. If no one's around to fix the castle, it should eventually fall apart and that should mean the end of the Keepers, too. Until then, you both need to stay well away."

"No!" cried Max, aghast. He wasn't some useless lump who needed to be looked after. "I'm here to help you! There's no way we're leaving you here!"

"You've got to," said Bram firmly. "All I want now is for you two to get out of here alive."

Bram had a desperate look in his eyes.

"Promise me you'll escape," he said urgently. "Promise."

"All right," said Kit, looking unnerved. "I promise."

"And you, Max?"

Max felt sick at the idea of leaving Bram. He'd spent so much time wondering how to rescue his grandfather from the castle. He had never imagined that it would end up like this.

"It's the only way," Bram repeated. "Promise me."

But Max found that he couldn't do it.

Bram gave a sigh.

"I'm sorry, Max," he said, then he flung open the door to the mass of flickering shadows.

"I'll do it," he bellowed. "Tell her I'll spellstop the castle right now!"

He turned to Max and Kit, his expression deadly serious.

"As soon as I'm out of sight, get out of here as fast as you can – do you understand? You don't have much time."

Max nodded mutely, and Bram clapped him on the shoulder. Kit gave a small sob.

"Look after yourselves," he said gruffly. Then he looked straight at Max, and his face softened.

"I'm proud of you," he said. "You'll make a great spellstopper."

Then Bram strode off bravely down the corridor, with all the shadows whirling around him. Max watched his grandfather go, unable to believe what was about to happen.

21

"We've got to try and escape," whispered Kit, once Bram's footsteps had died away and the shadow people had disappeared. "It's what Bram wants."

Max nodded, not trusting himself to speak. He peered up and down the passageway, checking for any lingering shadows. But there was no sign of them.

"Let's do it then," he said heavily.

They hurried back through the maze of corridors and empty enchanted rooms. Every time they came to a corner, they peered around it, making sure that the way in front of them was clear.

Max felt numb after what had just happened with Bram, and he could tell that Kit felt the same. Neither of them said much – it was not the right time. All they could do now was to follow Bram's last request and escape from the castle. Max forced himself to keep moving forwards, focusing on the way ahead.

They tiptoed down a steep flight of steps to the ground floor, not knowing that a shadow had appeared behind them.

"It's just across from here," whispered Kit, darting down a narrow side passage that ran alongside the dining hall.

Max followed her, straining his eyes to see in the dim light. There were very few candles in this thin slip of a corridor. If either of them had glanced back, they would have seen that there was now a mass of shadows creeping out of the darkness behind them. But neither of them did. They were too busy looking for the way into the sewers.

Kit was examining the stone floor carefully.

"It's just here," she hissed and hurried forwards. There, at the side of the passage, was a square stone slab. It looked exactly like the rest of the floor, except that it had a small iron handle set into it.

"Help me lift it," she said, and they both seized the handle and hauled up the slab, revealing a gaping black hole.

"There's actually some handholds down there," said Kit, pointing. "That's how I managed to climb up. I just hope you'll be able to hold your breath for long enough, once we're in the water. If I'm able to transform again, I should be fine."

She broke off, looking at Max, who had backed away from the edge of the hole.

"What's the matter?"

"We can't just leave Bram. No matter what he said."

"Once we're out of here, we'll get help and come back," said Kit. "There's loads of people in the village who hate Leandra. We know of a way in now."

"It'll take too long," said Max. "Bram could be dead by then."

He broke off suddenly. Kit was staring at something just over his shoulder, her eyes wide. He glanced around and saw the huge shadowy shapes rearing up behind him. More appeared behind Kit – there were dozens now, surrounding both of them.

"Quick!" Kit cried, grabbing his arm, and they plunged forwards, trying to escape into the safety of the tunnel, but the shadows swooped upon them and wrapped their inky forms around them, enveloping them in darkness.

Max couldn't see – he could barely breathe in the suffocating blackness that swirled around him like a tornado. It scooped him up and whirled him along, so that his feet skimmed the ground. He had no sense of the direction that they were going in – it was like being caught in a nightmare. He tried to struggle against the blackness, to push it away, but his fists simply sank into the air. It was impossible to fight a being without a body, that was made of nothing but shadow.

Finally, his horrible journey came to an abrupt stop. The shadow people unwrapped themselves from him, and he was left, dizzy and disorientated, at a familiar door. Kit spun to a halt beside him, looking green.

"I think I'm going to be sick," she groaned. "It's the second time that's happened this evening."

Then Leandra burst through the door, looking furious. She frowned when she saw them.

"Did you really think you'd manage to escape?" she said, as the shadows whispered around her.

Kit gave a groan and puked all over the corridor. It splattered everywhere, narrowly missing Leandra's boots.

There was a horrible pause as Leandra looked at them both in disgust.

"Finished?" she spat.

Kit, who was still looking rather green, glared at her weakly.

"You may as well come in," Leandra continued. "You might liven the old man up a bit. Now he'll see it's either him or you."

Fear gripped Max as Leandra beckoned them inside the room that was full of magic, and he saw his grandfather slumped at the edge of the marble floor.

"Bram!" he yelled, and dashed towards his grandfather, Kit close behind him. "What happened?"

Bram didn't reply. He seemed to be finding it difficult to speak, and his breath was coming in great rattling gasps. When he saw Max and Kit, he clutched his hand to his chest and looked as if he had been stabbed.

"Thought you'd got out," he whispered, so faintly that Max could hardly hear him.

"What did you do to him?" asked Kit, facing Leandra.

"He collapsed almost as soon as he touched the rock," she replied, sounding annoyed. "The minute he gets his breath back, he can have another go."

"You can't make him try again!" said Max in fury. "Look at him! He's not well."

"I don't care," replied Leandra. "Bram is going to fix the castle. Right now."

Max knew that Bram couldn't survive another encounter with something as powerful as that stone.

There was no way that he would be able to let the magic that kept an entire castle afloat run through him while he was in this state. Max looked across the marble floor at the shimmering opal rock, and to his surprise, he felt oddly drawn to it.

"I'll do it," he said, looking at Leandra. Bram seemed to be barely conscious. He couldn't let his grandfather die in front of him. Anything would be better than that.

"Go ahead," she said, shrugging. "I don't care who fixes the castle. As long as someone does."

Max focused on trying to empty his mind, to ready himself. It wasn't easy. A million unhappy, frightened and dismal thoughts were fighting for space, wanting to overwhelm his brain. He could feel them crowding around the edges of his mind, like the shadow people who were lurking just outside the door.

There was the thought that he couldn't possibly do this, that he was never going to manage a task as ridiculously huge as this one. He was just Max, a boy who until recently couldn't even touch a light switch without electrocuting himself. His mind unhelpfully provided him with countless memories of the many, many things he'd broken – from the school computers to his best friend's games console. No wonder his mother always looked so anxious. He thought again of how he'd destroyed her brand-new car – breaking it had been bad enough, but the fact that he'd fainted as well made it even worse. There were a million examples of how useless he was.

He moved towards the patterned floor but then took a step backwards again.

"What's the matter?" whispered Kit, coming over to him.

"What if I can't manage it?"

"Max, you're the only person who has even the slightest chance of being able to do this. Think about everything you've done – remember what happened in the tunnel. You're stronger than you think."

Max remembered how Bram had said he'd never heard of anyone being able to spellstop a ley line before, and he felt a bit better. Perhaps Kit was right – perhaps he did stand a chance. He took a step forwards onto the marble floor and at once felt the energy radiating outwards from the glowing rock in the centre. The air was crackling with it.

"Max," croaked Bram again, then doubled over with pain as Leandra gave him a sharp kick.

"Get on with it," she said impatiently, scowling at Max.

Max turned his back on both of them and tried again to focus.

Although he knew how to spellstop, he couldn't help but feel overwhelmed. The challenge ahead was terrifying. But, as he stared at the stone, his skin prickling from the magic that sparked and fizzed though the air, he realized that whether he succeeded or not, he was going to try anyway. He felt stronger, somehow, once that thought had occurred to him. Worrying was just chewing over a problem until it ate you up. It couldn't change anything. There was no point in dwelling upon the past or worrying about the future, when there was a chance to do something right now, in the present.

With this realization, Max felt his mind clear. It was like going up in a plane, when you get to the bright blue sky that's always waiting just above the clouds. He felt completely calm as he walked forwards, across the circles and symbols that now seemed to be moving beneath his feet, and placed both his hands firmly upon the great glowing rock that was the heart of the castle's magic.

Max felt a huge wave of energy flow through him. It felt pleasantly warm and made him feel more alive, somehow, as if every cell in his body was more awake than usual. He could tell that the castle's magic was unbalanced – the excess energy seemed to ping and jump through his veins – but somehow it didn't hurt. He closed his eyes and let it swirl through him. There was a moment when he thought it was working, that he was draining the magic away. Then a blaze of sharp red light flashed across his vision, almost blinding him. It broke Max's concentration and in that instant he was hit by a violent force so strong that it flung him right into the air. He crashed to the ground, half stunned by the impact. The castle's magic was fighting back.

He scrambled to his feet, and staggered towards the stone again.

He was vaguely aware that the others were shouting at him, but he didn't hear what they were saying. He was too focused on the task that lay ahead. This time, when he placed his hands on the stone, he didn't flinch, even though he knew what was coming. Flashes of blood-red light blazed before his eyes and every part of him was screaming with pain, but he didn't budge. His whole being was focused on draining the energy out of the castle, and gradually he felt it change as it came under his control, slowly seeping out of the building and fading away into the atmosphere. Everything felt lighter, somehow. There was still plenty of magic inside the stone

– he could feel it. But it was no longer the unstable crackling energy of before.

Unsure of what to do now, Max blinked and opened his eyes. The deep red flame that had been flickering inside the rock had faded to a soft pink. Leandra was studying the markings on the floor, which had changed colour too, and rearranged themselves.

"You've done it!" she said and she gave him a dazzling smile. She flicked her finger and a glowing flame appeared at the tip of her sharp silvery nail.

"Excellent," she said, and blew it out. "You've rebalanced it perfectly."

Max was no longer touching the rock, but he could still feel its energy coursing through him. He felt slightly dazed – it was a bit like the feeling you get when you're woken up midway through a dream.

"Can we leave now?" he asked.

"Fine," she said, shrugging. "You can crawl back through the sewers if you like."

"But Bram can't do that!" exclaimed Kit. "He's not well."

"Don't talk to me like that," snapped Leandra.

She gave a little flick of her finger and instantly flames licked at Kit's long hair. Her hair didn't catch alight, but it shrivelled and singed, and a horrible smell of burning filled the room.

Kit gasped as she clutched at a handful of her blackened hair and it came away in her hands.

"You're not going to change, are you?" asked Max, who was still standing beside the stone. "You're just going to carry on terrorizing everybody."

"Why shouldn't I?" replied Leandra. "I never asked to be stuck here, bound to this castle my entire life. If I can't be happy, I'm going to make sure that no one else is either."

Bram had struggled to his feet and was staggering over to Kit, who seemed frozen with shock, still clutching a handful of burned hair. But Max hadn't moved. He realized that he hadn't yet finished. If he walked away now, nothing would have changed. Leandra would carry on persecuting everybody, and the castle would continue to cast a shadow across the whole of Yowling. Max decided that he was going to attempt what Bram had said was impossible. He was going to completely spellstop the castle. He took a deep, steadying breath and placed his hands back on the rock.

This time, it was even harder than before. The castle clearly didn't want to be spellstopped. Pain shot up his arms again, and through his body. It felt unbearable. There was so much magic flooding through him that Max's legs began to tremble and give way. He threw himself forwards, so he was half-slumped over the rock, clasping it with both hands as the ancient, embedded energy that pulsed through it seeped into him, and little by little, diffused into the surrounding air and vanished. His teeth were clenched with the sheer agony of it and every fibre of his body felt like it was on fire. But something seemed to be happening. The swirling colours inside the rock were fading. Dazed, Max watched as the light drained away and the rock became dull and opaque, until it looked just like a lump of ordinary grey stone, no different to that of the surrounding walls. Then, with a sharp crack, it split in two, and the marble floor shattered into a hundred pieces.

Throughout this, Max had been dimly aware of Leandra screaming at him to stop, but she didn't seem to be able to get near him, as the energy surrounding him was so strong, almost like a force field. He'd looked up as the stone's colour faded away, and seen that Leandra was hunched over as if she was in pain. As the stone broke, she gave a long loud cry that became the call of an owl. She whirled around and her long black hair and floating chiffon dress became feathers. Max collapsed onto the shattered stone floor, breathing heavily, and stared in shock as Leandra was transformed, clearly against her will, into an owl. The diamond necklace clattered to the ground.

With a screech, the owl flew past them, and down the dark corridors without a backwards glance. And from somewhere in the castle, came a low rumbling noise, like the sound of thunder.

22

For a moment, Max stayed where he was, slumped in the middle of the floor, still reeling from what had just happened. His muscles seemed to have turned to jelly, and as he scrambled to his feet, he stumbled and almost fell over.

"Are you all right?" cried Kit as she hurried over to him, her soot-streaked face alight with worry.

"I think so," he said, taking a couple of deep breaths, trying to steady himself. He stared at the broken marble floor and the shattered stone, still in shock.

"You've done it!" croaked Bram, who was somehow staggering towards him, a look of absolute astonishment on his face. "You've spellstopped the castle! I didn't think it was possible."

"What do you think happened to Leandra?" asked Max, picking up the diamond necklace and putting it in his pocket. "Will she stay as an owl?"

"I'd say so," said Bram, who was swaying slightly, as if he was in danger of falling over again. "She'll have to join the rest of the old Keepers now. And it doesn't look like there'll be another one in her place, either, not after what you've done."

Kit, meanwhile, had slipped through the door into the passageway beyond.

"So there's good news and there's bad news," she said, coming back inside. "The good news is that all the shadow people seem to have vanished."

"And the bad news?" asked Max.

"The castle's falling down."

"Should've guessed," said Bram, and he made his way stiffly to the door, wincing with every step. "Now you've taken away the magic, there's nothing keeping the place together. We need to get out. Right now."

"Let's try the sewer again," said Kit. "It's our best chance."

They hurried back through the corridors, the two of them helping Bram, who was still unsteady on his feet. The staircase crumbled as they went down it, the stone falling away beneath them. They stumbled forwards, as all around, the walls started to buckle and disintegrate.

"The whole castle's going to go!" yelled Max, who had Bram's arm around his shoulder and was half-supporting his grandfather as they hurried forwards. He wished Bram could move a bit faster. If they didn't get out soon, they'd all be crushed. But Bram was barely able to get over the gaping holes in the floorboards, or clamber across the fallen walls, as they made their way through rooms that were disintegrating around them.

In the end, they didn't need to go down the sewer. There was a great, deafening roar and an entire section of the outer wall collapsed, tumbling into the sea, and opening up a giant gaping hole in the side of the building, a full three storeys high.

Then, with a huge, stomach-churning groan, the castle itself began to sink, as if the rocks that it stood on had crumbled. The sea flooded in, swirling round their ankles and rising rapidly with every passing second.

"Come on!" said Max, still supporting Bram as the three of them splashed forwards, through the hole in the castle wall.

"Are you going to be able to swim?" he asked, looking at his grandfather apprehensively. He had a feeling that Bram was much weaker than he was letting on.

"Be fine," grunted Bram, staring into the waves.

"I'll be able to help him," said Kit, speaking to Max in a low voice. "Hopefully I'll transform again once we're in the water."

"Hopefully?" echoed Max, looking at Kit in shock. "You don't know?"

"I've only done it once before, haven't I?" she said defensively. "I'm not sure if I'll be able to do it again."

The waves were lapping about their knees now as the castle continued to sink. Rocks and slates and chunks of masonry crashed about them, splashing into the waves as the building slowly fell apart, with groans and creaks and shuddering sighs.

"We'll have to risk it," said Max. "We're going to end up in the sea whatever we do."

"Now?" asked Kit, as more rubble rained down.

Max nodded.

"Now," he said. He and Kit seized Bram firmly by the arms and the three of them launched themselves forwards into the sea.

Max sank down below the waves, and the salt water filled his nose and stung his eyes. He tried to swim up to the surface, but Bram was thrashing about instead of swimming, pulling Max further down. Max struggled, desperately trying to keep them both afloat, but it was no use. They were sinking still further, and he felt as if his lungs were about to burst.

Then something was pushing both of them upwards, so they were rising up through the water, and finally Max felt his head break the surface and he took a great, spluttering gulp of the cool night air. Bram's head was above the water too, and he was breathing, but seemed not to be fully conscious. Then Max saw the brown head of a seal bobbing in the waves beside them and he realized that Kit, true to her word, had rescued them both.

"Kit?" he spluttered, half expecting her to reply, but the seal just ducked under the waves and nudged Bram forwards, in the direction of the shore. There was a deafening crash and another corner of the castle fell into the sea, making the waves rough and choppy. Kit was steadily helping Bram onwards, but the current was strong, and the shore looked very far away. Max realized that they were in as much danger as ever. He kept scanning the water, knowing that it was highly likely that the mugfish would attack them.

Their situation was made worse by the fact that Bram was too weak to swim unaided. Max was a reasonable swimmer, but not good enough to battle his way through open water while dragging a fully grown man. Kit was doing the brunt of the work, guiding Bram along, but their progress was slow.

Max could feel himself getting tired, but even though he kept his eyes fixed on the glimmering lights of the village, they didn't seem to be getting any closer. Behind them, he could hear the constant rumble of collapsing rock, as the castle slowly disintegrated. It groaned and shuddered as if it was a living thing, and the sea around it churned and bubbled as great chunks of hewn stone hit the water, creating endless lurching waves that rippled out to where they swam.

Max was beginning to wonder if they would ever get to safety. He forced himself to keep on going, even though his arms and legs felt like lead, and each breath became harder and harder. And then something fastened its rubbery jaws around his ankle. A mugfish had found them.

He tried to kick his foot free, but more fish were circling. As soon as Max had dislodged one, another six took its place, and he kept being pulled under the water. They'd fastened upon him now, and were chewing their way through his clothes, trying to get hold of his flesh.

Then, miraculously, he heard a voice.

"Ahoy there!" it called.

A boat was gliding towards them. Max barely registered it at first – he was too busy trying to free himself from the fish – but then a pair of large, webbed hands seized him under the arms and hauled him into a very familiar boat.

"Yurp," said Tom with a grin, as he pulled the remaining mugfish off Max and tossed them back into the sea.

The Captain was there too, wrapping a blanket around Bram's shoulders with his ghostly fingers. Kit, still in seal form, was bobbing along beside the boat.

"How did you know we were out here?" gasped Max.

"We didn't," said the Captain. "I'd spotted that something was going on at the castle and I got Tom to take me out for a better look. Then we saw some lost souls bobbing in the water, and bless me if it wasn't you lot!"

"But I thought your boat was ruined," said Max, turning to Tom.

"I patched it up this morning," said Kit. She had transformed back into a human and was clambering into the boat, as if nothing out of the ordinary had occurred. "I thought it would be better if *I* did it this time."

"By Jove!" cried the Captain, clutching a ghostly hand to his chest. "I didn't know you were a selkie, young Kit."

"Neither did I," replied Kit, and she smiled from ear to ear.

Still looking rather shaken, the Captain went to pick up an oar, but Tom promptly grabbed it off him.

"Right you are, Tom," he said, surrendering the oar in a slightly sheepish manner and settling back into the prow of the boat. "Let's get them back to shore."

"Look!" cried Kit, pointing.

Max twisted around on the bench and saw the castle silhouetted under the light of the full moon. It had sunk almost halfway under the waves, which gave it an oddly squat appearance, especially since so many of the towers had already crumbled. He couldn't believe that he had caused all of that. It seemed unbelievable – the sheer scale of it.

"Didn't I always say you'd make a brilliant spellstopper?" said Bram, who seemed to have recovered from the shock and was looking slightly better. He gave Max a wobbly grin. "But that was truly incredible. You've not just saved me, but you've freed the whole village. Things are going to be very different in Yowling from now on."

Max felt as if he might burst with happiness. The relief was overwhelming. There was another distant rumble and they all watched as the huge stone building folded in on itself, crumpling as easily as a house made of playing cards, and slid beneath the waves. The ripples of it rocked the little rowing boat, and they lurched from side to side. When the water settled, Max looked over towards the castle once more, but there was no longer any trace of it. The only sign that it had ever been there was the flock of owls, wheeling about in circles over the spot where it once stood.

23

It was a hot August afternoon, and Max and Kit were sitting on the beach at Yowling. It had been almost three weeks since they had escaped from the castle, and lots of things had changed since then. Some of the changes were small, like the fact that Kit now wore her auburn hair in a short bob instead of it falling down below her shoulders. The bottom of it had been so badly singed that she'd ended up having to cut it off.

"I don't mind, though," Kit had said, ever practical. "It means I don't have to tie it back if I'm fixing something."

The most obvious change was the bay itself. Now that the castle was gone, everything seemed more open and cheerful. The owls had all scattered into the woods, and even the rocks that guarded the mouth of the cove looked less daunting. Boats bobbed on the water, and Omar had parked his new van right on the seafront, where a long line of customers were queuing patiently for ice cream. That was the biggest change of all – the people. Since Leandra's departure, the residents of Yowling had ventured out of their homes. The village was no longer eerily empty – instead, it was full of life.

"Hello, Max," said a moon-faced man in a squashed straw sunhat, who was walking a small, strangely hairy creature on a lead, as if it were a dog. Or rather, the creature appeared to be walking him – it was making a shrill, squeaking sound and scampering off towards the dunes, dragging the man swiftly after it.

"Who was that?" asked Max, as the peculiar pair headed off into the distance. "And how did he know my name?"

"Word spreads quickly in Yowling," said Kit. "Everyone knows what happened in the castle by now. They know it's thanks to you there's no more Keepers."

"I still can't believe I sank the entire castle," said Max, staring at the sea. "Bram's really excited about it. I don't think he's too happy about me going back to London – he says I need to carry on spellstopping."

"What do you want to do?"

"Stay here, of course," said Max.

The idea of having to go back to his old life in London, where nothing exciting ever seemed to happen, was hanging over him like a cloud. He was acutely aware that the summer holidays were nearly over, and his days in Yowling were rapidly running out. He and Kit had been managing the spellstopping business while Bram recovered. It had been really fun – they had dealt with all sorts of things, from subduing a flying bathtub to returning the stolen diamond necklace to its owner. Max realized that this had been the best summer of his life, even though it had also been the most terrifying.

In the distance, he could see the long scaly back of something large and lizard-like, which was propelling itself through the water like a crocodile.

"Is that the thing from the tunnel?" he asked, changing the subject.

"I hope not," said Kit, peering at it. "That's the last thing I need. After twelve whole years, I finally figure out how to transform at the exact same time that another monster ends up in the cove."

"Did you ever work out how you were suddenly able to do it?"

"Dad reckons it might have been because I stopped thinking so much about it," she said thoughtfully. "After what happened when I was little – that time I nearly drowned – I just don't think I was ever comfortable enough in the water to be able to transform. Even when I jumped into that pool after Eppie, I remember worrying about whether we'd drown. It was only when I waded out into the sea, after the owls had taken you, that I genuinely didn't think about it. And that was when it finally happened."

"That's amazing," said Max, grinning at her. "I suppose it was a bit like me figuring out how to spellstop – as soon as I stopped holding myself back, I could do it."

"I guess we've both learned a lot this summer," said Kit, returning his smile.

They were silent for a few moments. Max looked out to sea, and Kit drew a pattern in the sand with her finger.

"So, my mother's going to open up a nursery to sell her plants," she said. "She's already found the perfect place, just at the edge of the village. She feels like she can finally do it, now that Leandra's gone."

"That's fantastic news," said Max. "Did you hear that Pearl's back too? She's about to reopen her cafe. She came over yesterday and was telling us all about it."

"What's that noise?" asked Kit, scrunching up her face. Max could hear it too. It was the sound of a car – the first one that he had ever heard in the village. The road that led to Yowling ended there, which deterred any passing traffic, and because the streets were so steep and narrow and full of steps, the few residents who owned vehicles kept them parked a short distance away. But here was a car, coming right along the seafront.

It stopped on the road, just above where Max and Kit were sitting on the beach, and a woman rolled down the car window and stuck her head out.

"It's my mother!" cried Max, in surprise. It looked as if she was driving the very same car that he had broken.

"I thought she wasn't picking you up until the end of the week," said Kit, turning round to look at her.

"So did I," he replied, getting up.

"Maybe she's here for Bram's birthday dinner tonight? Go and speak to her – I'll see you later."

Max left Kit on the beach and padded his way up across the sand until he reached his mother.

She had got out of the car and was standing at the edge of the road, at the point where it turned into sand. She was gazing out to sea as if she couldn't believe her eyes.

"Mum?" said Max.

She came over and hugged him, very tightly, and for a very long time.

"I've missed you so much," she said, letting go of him at last. "I didn't know you were down on the beach. I haven't even been to Bram's yet. After he told me what had happened with the castle, I wanted to see it for myself."

She glanced across the seafront, towards the village.

"Apart from the castle, it looks just the same. I've missed it."

"Why didn't you ever tell me about it?" asked Max. "If you'd grown up in this world, why didn't you let me know it existed?"

"Because I was never part of it," she said sadly. "I had no special power, so I wasn't like the rest of the villagers. I was never going to be a spellstopper. And after Leandra attacked me, I really didn't want to stay. I wanted to make a new life for myself, and I felt even more strongly about that when you came along. I just wanted to keep you safe. It wasn't until it became clear that you needed to be trained that I had to admit that I couldn't keep you away any longer."

"You could have given me some warning," said Max. "I thought I was cursed."

"I didn't know what was going on either, at first. Remember, I never showed any signs of it. And once I'd figured it out, I still didn't want you to come here. It was only when Bram warned me that you'd be in serious danger as an untrained spellstopper that I realized I'd have to give in."

She sighed, and looked at Max, her face crumpling a little.

"I'm sorry," she said. "I didn't mean to make life harder for you. I was just trying to do the right thing."

"It's okay," said Max, and he smiled at her. "It all worked out in the end."

His mother smiled back at him, and for once, the perpetually worried expression on her face vanished.

"Shall I drive you back to the farmhouse?" she asked.

Max nodded.

"I've got your gloves—" she began, but Max had already opened the front door on the passenger side and got in. His mother gaped at him in astonishment.

"I'm fine with electricity now," he said, as he closed the door. "I told you, remember?"

She went round and got into the driver's seat, still looking slightly stunned.

"How did you get the car fixed?" asked Max. "I thought they said it was impossible."

"It's a new one – they ended up replacing it. They thought that there must have been some sort of defect with the battery. I mean, it didn't sound great, the fact that the car knocked my son unconscious. I can see why they wanted to smooth it over."

Max grinned.

"I'll try not to do it again," he said.

"Please don't," said his mother weakly.

She started the car and they drove up the lane to the farmyard. Bram came out to meet them. He had almost completely recovered in the last couple of weeks, and was nearly back to his old self. Bram and Max's mother had spoken on the phone quite a lot recently, and he was beaming from ear to ear when he saw his daughter and Max arrive together.

"Happy birthday!" she called, as soon as she spotted him.

"Knew you'd come round in the end," said Bram, helping her out of the car. "I'll give you a hand with your things."

Max glanced into the back of the car and saw that it was packed full of bags.

"How long are you planning on staying?" he asked, but his mother had already gone into the farmhouse, and his voice was drowned out by the happy barking of the dogs.

It felt as if hardly any time had passed before the first guests started arriving for Bram's birthday dinner. Kit arrived with her parents and sister in tow, and was swiftly followed by Pearl, who was staggering along carrying a large box, which turned out to contain an enormous birthday cake. The dogs greeted her with delight and knocked the box straight out of her hands. It was only by sheer luck that Max grabbed it before they had a chance to dive in. Then the Captain arrived, accompanied by Tom. Max had invited them both, as a way of saying thank you for pulling them out of the sea that night at the castle.

They all squashed together around the long farmhouse table.

"So what are we having for dinner then?" asked the Captain, patting his stomach in a very unghostlike way.

"I'm starving," announced Kit. She looked so expectant and happy that Max genuinely felt sorry for her. She had no idea what was coming next.

"Bram insisted on cooking dinner himself," he said, feeling like he should warn her. "We couldn't stop him."

Kit's face fell.

"No," she whispered. "It can't be…"

"Stew!" announced Bram, carrying an enormous vat of steaming brown gunk over to the table.

All the guests gagged. It smelled exactly like all of Bram's stews – utterly disgusting.

"There's plenty for everyone," said Bram, going round the table and slopping stew onto plates. "Don't feel like you have to hold back."

Max tried very hard not to laugh as he saw the expressions on all the guests' faces. It seemed as if the real danger was that they wouldn't be able to hold back from being sick at the sheer sight of such a lumpy, rancid mess.

Despite the food, everybody seemed to be enjoying themselves. The three dogs possibly enjoyed themselves the most, as person after person discreetly tipped their stew onto the floor, where it was instantly polished off by Treacle, Sardine or Banana.

Afterwards, they all sang "Happy Birthday" to Bram, as Pearl brought the beautifully decorated cake over to the table, which blazed with an impressive number of candles. It took Bram six goes to blow them all out and afterwards he looked a little lightheaded.

It was lucky that the cake was so enormous, because everyone was still extremely hungry. Fortunately, after several fat wedges of apple cake, even Max felt stuffed. He looked around the table, at the happy, laughing faces, and felt a pang of sadness at the prospect of leaving. This felt like home now. He nudged his mother, who was sitting beside him, and she broke off her conversation with Pearl and turned to look at him.

"I don't want to go back," he said desperately. "I want to stay here."

"Good," said his mother, and Max stared at her in surprise.

"I thought we'd both settle here for a while," she said. "See how things go."

"Seriously?" spluttered Max, hardly able to believe what he was hearing. "We're going to live with Bram? Both of us?"

His mother nodded.

"That way you can carry on spellstopping," she said. "And I wanted a change anyway. Pearl's just offered me a job in her cafe."

"Does Bram know we're staying?" asked Max, and his mother laughed.

"Of course he does," she said. "It was his idea, actually."

At the other side of the table, Bram got to his feet and whacked a fork against his glass until everyone fell silent.

"Thanks to all of you for coming this evening," he said, looking around the table. "As I think you've all guessed from the amount of candles on that cake, I'm now in what's known as the prime of my life. And I've been thinking that it's about time for me to retire."

There was a murmur around the table and Kit turned to Max in shock.

"He can't!" she gasped.

Max felt his heart sink too. For a moment it had seemed as if everything was going perfectly, but if Bram was going to retire, that would put an end to the spellstopping.

"Luckily for me, I've got two apprentices," Bram continued. "And I'm planning on handing the business over to them – if they're happy about it, of course."

Max stared at Kit, speechless. She stared back at him, looking equally overwhelmed. Then, as it slowly sank in, they started to grin.

"What do you say?" said Bram. "Is it a yes?"

They both spoke at once, not even needing to think about it.

"Yes!"

Everyone around the table clapped and cheered. Bram made his way over to his new apprentices.

"Should've have asked you before," he said, a roguish smile on his face. "But I couldn't resist surprising you. And to be honest, I didn't see either of you saying no. I'll still be here to give you a hand if you need it. But I reckon you'll make a good team – Kit can repair anything and, Max, you're the best spellstopper I've ever seen. I know you'll be able to carry on the business. You'll do a fantastic job."

He clapped each of them on the shoulder, then moved along the table to speak to Kit's parents, who seemed somewhat bewildered that their twelve-year-old daughter had suddenly inherited half of Bram's business.

"This is crazy," said Kit, beaming at Max.

"I know," he replied. "But it's going to be a lot of fun."

Max looked around the table, at the array of friendly faces, and was enveloped in a warm glow of happiness. In just one short summer, his life had changed beyond anything he'd ever dreamed of, and the world felt like a much bigger and more wonderful place to be. Once, Max had believed he was cursed. Now, he felt like the luckiest person alive.

He glanced out of the window to where the workshop stood, a light still glinting in the window. There was a whole pile of things waiting to be spellstopped, and more adventures to be had. They'd start tomorrow, Max decided. He smiled broadly, unable to contain his excitement. He could hardly wait.

Discover more pockets
of magic that hide just out
of sight, with a sneak peek at
the next adventure from the
imagination of
Cat Gray

Chapter 1

All parents are challenging on some level, but Pip Ruskin's parents were off the scale. Their unrelenting weirdness had blighted the first twelve years of his life and it seemed as if things were about to get even worse.

"It's a dream come true," sighed Mrs Ruskin, as she stretched out in the front seat of their battered turquoise car, a large jar of home-made pickles in her lap.

"No, it isn't," corrected Pip. He was squashed in the back seat, along with a dozen bulging suitcases. "I don't want to live in London."

"When I was your age, I'd have given anything to live in the middle of a city like this," said his father, grinning at him madly in the rear-view mirror. He was so excited, he looked like he was about to explode. "Isn't it wonderful?"

Pip stared miserably out at the never-ending traffic jam. Massive grey buildings reared up on either side of the wide road, and people hurried through the rain, their hoods up or hiding behind umbrellas. For the millionth time that day, Pip wished they hadn't had to move.

It wasn't that Pip liked their old life in Norwich. It was more that he had learned how to deal with it. Living with Mr and Mrs Ruskin was not exactly easy, and Pip had become an expert at damage limitation.

There were the obvious things that made them different to other people's parents, like his mother's hair, which was silvery grey and so long that she could sit on it, and her round little glasses that made her look like an owl. There was his father's yellow corduroy suit, which he wore every single day and was so bright he had once been mistaken for a clown. Some things were less noticeable at first, but still not great, like his father's habit of singing to himself or his mother's extreme forgetfulness, or the way that his parents held hands and kissed in public – not the peck-on-the-cheek kind of kiss, but the slobbery sort that goes on for too long and makes other people stare. Individually, none of these things were too bad, but when you put them all together it became a problem. The more his parents stood out, the harder it was for Pip to fit in. In fact, fitting in, or, at the very least, not having anyone notice him, was Pip's main ambition in life.

"How about a fermented Brussels sprout, darling?" said Mrs Ruskin. She flipped open the glass lid of the pickle jar and instantly a hideous smell, like rotten vinegary eggs, filled the car. She twisted round, waving the jar under Pip's nose. He choked, trying not to be sick, and opened the window. He stuck his head out and breathed in the petrol fumes gratefully.

"Don't you want one?" asked his mother, still holding out the reeking jar.

"I'm not hungry," said Pip, then felt bad when he saw her face fall.

"But I'd love one anyway," he amended. He prised a slimy green Brussels sprout out of the jar as his stomach lurched again and the bile rose in his throat.

Mrs Ruskin beamed at him. She was a great believer in gut-friendly food. All their meals involved large quantities of every sort of fermented vegetable you can imagine. Even worse, she insisted on making Pip a packed lunch every day. After five long hours of sweating away in Pip's schoolbag, Mrs Ruskin's carefully prepared lunchbox of mackerel, broccoli and home-made pickles inevitably transformed into a hand grenade of appalling smelliness. Pip dreaded opening the lid. It was like setting off a stink bomb – the ripe bin-lorry stench would hit him full in the face then whoosh outwards, spreading across the classroom and causing everybody to do a stadium wave of nose-wrinkling, face-scrunching and gagging noises. After the first few times, Pip learned that it was better if he ate his lunch alone, in the furthest corner of the schoolyard. With lunches like his, it had been impossible to make any friends. But his mother looked so surprised and upset whenever he mentioned he didn't like her food that he had long since dropped the subject.

He tossed the Brussels sprout out of the car window when no one was looking, and wondered what his new school would be like. At least he didn't have to start until after the half-term break at Halloween – he had almost a month of freedom before he had to figure out how to blend in all over again. He was pretty certain that his parents would be as peculiar in London as they had been in Norwich.

The traffic lights turned green and they lurched forwards. The pile of suitcases toppled over and crashed on top of Pip. By the time he'd freed himself they were heading through a maze of city streets.

"Nearly there," said Mr Ruskin, squinting at the satnav. They went past a large auction house, its windows plastered with images of treasures they'd sold, past galleries displaying gold-framed paintings and strangely shaped sculptures, and office buildings with revolving glass doors. It was not the sort of place where families lived, but Mrs Ruskin was a scientist and had got a new job teaching science in a London university, which meant they all had to move home just six weeks into the new school year. Pip's father had come across an advert for a shop to rent in one of London's most famous antiques districts, which had a flat above it. The rent was very cheap, and as it had always been Mr Ruskin's ambition to open an antiques shop, they'd taken on the lease without even having seen the place and promptly booked a removal van.

"We're here!" announced Mr Ruskin. He looked round expectantly, then frowned. "At least, it says we're here."

"We can't be," replied Mrs Ruskin. "The shop's in Elbow Alley and we're still on Magwitch Street."

Leaving his parents puzzling over the satnav, Pip opened the car door and climbed out, rubbing his arm from where the suitcases had bruised him. It was a Sunday and the street was completely deserted. The offices were closed and so was the auction house, their windows dark. The only place that was lit up was a grand-looking gallery, where two huge old portraits stood in the windows, illuminated against a blood-red background. One of the paintings was of a stern, pale man in a ruff, the other of a woman who looked remarkably like a poodle.

Pip pushed at the gallery door, intending to ask for directions, but it didn't open. There was a bell, but something stopped him from pressing the button. Perhaps it was the unfriendly expressions on the pair of portraits, but the place felt intimidating. As he backed away, he spotted something. An archway was sandwiched between the side of the gallery and the office building on the other side, so narrow and tucked away that you'd hardly notice it was there.

Beyond the tunnel of the arch, there was a narrow little street, lined with shops. It looked like it belonged to a different time. The buildings were high and teetering, looming towards each other. Billows of steam from an air-vent swirled about like mist. A painted pub sign swung creakily in the autumn breeze. Pip spotted a street sign fixed a little way down the dark passage. It was Elbow Alley. He stared for a moment in surprise, unable to believe that this peculiar place was his new home.

His parents had got out of the car now and were gazing around Magwitch Street in their usual way – his mother looked distracted and dreamy, as if her mind was on other things, while his father was bouncing up and down on the soles of his feet, as if he couldn't contain his excitement.

"It's down here!" called Pip. He was too intrigued to wait for them, so he went on ahead, through the archway, and into the shadowy alley.

Join Pip as he meets the magical
creatures who hide in Elbow Alley
– including the mysterious
spirit-snatcher – in the next adventure
from Cat Gray, coming 2023

@Usborne
Usborne.com/fiction

Acknowledgements

When I started reading books, I thought they simply appeared, fully formed, as if by magic. But that isn't the case at all. *Spellstoppers* wouldn't exist if it wasn't for the help of lots of other people.

The main ones are Sarah Stewart and Rebecca Hill, my editors at Usborne, who encouraged me to write *Spellstoppers* when my idea was little more than a couple of paragraphs and then improved the manuscript immensely with their feedback. I'm lucky to work with two such brilliant editors, as well as the whole Usborne team, who are all absolutely wonderful.

I'm also extremely grateful to my agent Silvia Molteni for championing my writing in the most difficult circumstances. Silvia took me on in March 2020, and selling my work while stuck in Italy, in the middle of a global pandemic, was a truly superhuman feat. Lucy Irvine, another PFD agent, also deserves a mention for all her help.

A thank you to my sister Becky, and to my parents, Lucy and Nick, for reading *Spellstoppers* multiple times in draft form, which surely goes above and beyond the limits of parental affection.

And finally, an enormous thank you to my husband Tim, who was on the receiving end of a lot of brainstorming, and had the excellent idea of using a Komodo dragon as the basis for the monster in the tunnel. Komodo dragons aside, I couldn't have done it without him.